Geoffrey Benson was born and grew up in Cheshire. After graduating from Cambridge with a degree in Economics, he qualified as a Chartered Accountant and spent many years working in the profession. He is married with a grown-up son and divides his time between his homes in England and Spain.

To Pam and Dominic, the loves of my life.

Geoffrey Benson

BEN JONSON AND A CASE OF FRAUDULENT CONVERSION

AUSTIN MACAULEY PUBLISHERS™

LONDON • CAMBRIDGE • NEW YORK • SHARJAH

A CIP catalogue record for this title is available from the British Library.

ISBN 9781788483469 (Paperback)
ISBN 9781528918619 (Hardback)
ISBN 9781528918626 (Kindle e-book)
ISBN 9781528962384 (ePub e-book)

www.austinmacauley.com

First Published (2019)
Austin Macauley Publishers Ltd
25 Canada Square
Canary Wharf
London
E14 5LQ

This book is a work of fiction. Names, characters, businesses, organisations, places and events are either the product of the author's imagination or used fictitiously. Any resemblance to actual persons, living or dead, events or locales is entirely coincidental.

To the Guixolenc Writers Group of Sant Feliu, without whose encouragement this book may never have been written!

1. Ben Jonson and a Case of Fraudulent Conversion

"Things are seldom what they seem." *H.M.S Pinafore*

For almost as long as I can remember, I have had a fancy to perform the Nightmare Song from Gilbert & Sullivan's *Iolanthe*. You know, the one that goes on about "crossing the channel in something between a large bathing machine and a very small second-class carriage". I don't know what it is – perhaps the rhythm, or the words, or the combination of the two. There are other "patter songs" of course but they don't have the same allure, somehow.

I mentioned this in passing one afternoon to my Rottweiler of an office manager, Janet Mathieson. She gave me one of her steely looks.

'Can you sing?' she enquired.

I assured her that I was considered to have quite a reasonable voice. 'As it happens,' she went on, 'I'm in an operatic group, and we're always looking for new blood. Why don't you come to the auditions next week?'

And so it was that one wet Monday evening, I left my office and walked the few yards down the high street to the Church Hall. I pushed open the door and went through to a rather small side room. The group in question was the "County Amateur Operatic Society" to give the full name, or "CAOS" as it is abbreviated, the latter being unkindly felt in certain circles to accurately represent its performances.

In fact, I was auditioning for a role in "Patience" which was the upcoming production, but I felt it was a good start, so threw myself into what I considered to be a very creditable rendition of *If You're Anxious for to Shine.*

As I finished with a flourish, and curled myself (somewhat precariously) on top of a rickety trestle-table with a languid wave of the hand, there was a rather ominous silence from the assembled throng of would-be performers and the director, Clive Pettit. The latter, a plumpish, bustling man in his forties with a maiden-aunt campness about him, the sort that gives gay men a bad press, raised his hands and gave a solitary clap.

'Thank you *so* much, Ben,' he started. 'That was very…' here he seemed to struggle to find the right word, 'that was very…worthy,' he managed to end, rather lamely.

He went on, 'It's a loud voice, and I was thinking of something a bit, well, perhaps less *butch,* if you get my drift. Bunthorne is supposed to be an aesthete – a bit Oscar Wilde-ish, isn't he?'

I opened my mouth to protest, but Clive carried on. 'And also, if you don't mind me saying so, I envisaged someone a little younger? But I'm sure we can find you something in the chorus.'

As the chorus consists primarily of twenty lovesick maidens, I felt that this was definitely an offer I *could* refuse. I hurriedly made my excuses and headed for the door, where, to my surprise, I found Marcus, my partner, waiting. He gave me a sympathetic grin as I exited the room and followed me out.

'Ruddy man!' I exclaimed, referring to Clive. 'Jumped up little…'

Marcus put a hand on my shoulder.

'Hey, hey, steady on. Anyway, he may have a point. At least about your age, if not your voice.'

'Oh, thank you very much,' I retorted, 'with friends like you…'

We went out into the damp night air and walked without speaking the two hundred yards along the high street to our house. Well, I suppose, strictly speaking, *my* house, but for the last three years, Marcus has been there with me. It seems strange when I think about it, to find that, having been widowed at the age of forty and being on my own with two children for several years, that I have ended up as I am.

Finally having simmered down after my ignominious rebuff at the audition, I broke the silence and said, 'You're back early from Budapest. I didn't expect you tonight.'

Marcus replied shortly, 'We got through the presentation quicker than I thought, so I grabbed an earlier flight.'

He didn't seem eager to add any further detail, so I let it drop. These trips to Budapest have become a bit of an issue between us in the last few months...

But I see that I haven't introduced myself. Jonson's the name, Ben Jonson. Like the 17th century playwright. What were my parents thinking? My father had initially wanted me to have his middle name, John, but my mother had objected.

'John Jonson!' she had exclaimed, 'it would sound as though the poor child had a stammer!'

And so Ben it was. To be honest, I don't think it even crossed their minds that there was an illustrious namesake...

It's odd how life turns out, isn't it? I sort of drifted into accountancy after university. I suppose I did it really to please my parents: they were in thrall to the idea that "the professions" were the zenith of status and success, and perhaps that was true in their day.

And so I dutifully did my accountancy exams and then to my surprise, found that I actually enjoyed it. The idea of creating order out of chaos is I think deeply ingrained in me. Sometimes Marcus accuses me of having obsessive compulsive disorder. Well, perhaps I have, to an extent. It is true that I cannot leave a room if a drawer or wardrobe is not shut properly, and I hate items being left on the worktops in the kitchen, but I don't go so far as to have to align all the labels on the tins in the cupboard in the same direction like *he* does. But whatever, I discovered that the forensic accounting side was ideally suited to my attributes. The combination of accounting and legal procedures I find fascinating, although I have to admit, others, including Marcus, find it hard to understand.

Most of my work is fairly routine – accident and compensation claims mainly – but there are from time to time cases of a more invigorating kind. And so it was a week or so following my humiliating audition.

I was seated at my desk with a pile of files, issuing instructions to Sue, one of my trainee accountants. A fine looking girl of twenty-eight or so, with long dark hair and a figure that I think my mother would have described as buxom, Sue was yawning broadly.

I paused for a moment. 'Am I boring you, Sue?' I asked, a little curtly.

She looked up through heavy-lidded eyes. 'No, of course not, sorry, Ben.'

'Perhaps you should have an early night for once,' I said, still irritated. 'Stop burning the candle at both ends, eh?'

She gave a grimace, and said, 'I wish!' but before she could elaborate, the phone trilled. Sue answered it, then listened for a moment before passing it over to me, saying, 'Tom Bremner for you, Ben.'

I took the receiver off her and put it to my ear. Tom Bremner was the managing partner of a firm of solicitors, whose office was a few doors further down the high street. Tom and I have shared many a bottle of Vino Collapso at our local wine bar, Et Alia, and he has been a profitable source of business for my firm over the years.

'Got a good one for you today, old boy,' he began, 'suspected fraudulent conversion.' He rolled his tongue around the phrase as though sampling a particularly fragrant sauvignon blanc. 'I'll send the file across.'

He was as good as his word, and a few minutes later, a file was plonked on my desk.

I rapidly delegated the work I had, and gave orders not to be disturbed, then settled down to read. Flicking through the pages, my first surprise was to find that Tom's client was none other than my old nemesis, Clive Pettit. It seemed that he was employed as the financial controller of a moderately sized electrical contracting firm, Strand Electrics, and was accused of stealing, or in Tom's parlance, fraudulent conversion – the act of taking money or property that is not your own for illegal or dishonest purposes – to the tune of half a million or so.

The fraud, although skilfully done, was a relatively simple one. The bank details of a genuine, though no longer used, sub-contractor had been altered, and payments made on forged invoices to the "new" bank account. The scheme had come to light during the installation of new software, when a sharp member of the IT firm had noticed the unusual activity on this particular account. The CEO had been alerted and that is when the proverbial had hit the fan, at least as far as Clive Pettit was concerned. He had protested his innocence, but had been sent on indefinite gardening leave until enquiries were completed.

So my job was to show Clive was not the culprit. Trying to prove a negative is always a bit difficult: far better to prove a positive, that is, find the real villain. But nevertheless, there was still some routine work to be done, hopefully showing that unaccounted for funds were not flowing through Clive's bank accounts like a tsunami after an earthquake.

I worked steadily through the rest of the day, delegating some of the more prosaic tasks to one of my team. That is one of the benefits of being the boss – you can get rid of the boring bits of work. And although it was going to prove slightly awkward, I had to interview Clive himself, so a time was arranged for him to come to my office the next day.

The next afternoon, Clive duly arrived, with a bundle of documents which I had asked him to bring. He sat down at the meeting table I have in one corner of my room, and dabbed his forehead with a large handkerchief. His complexion, which has a vaguely greenish tinge at the best of times, was now positively verdant, and perspiration dripped off him in rivulets.

I murmured some sympathetic greeting, and in an attempt to lighten the mood, I tried some Gilbert & Sullivan. 'Well, here's a pretty how-de-do!'

His hands flew up. 'Oh, yes, "The Mikado",' he said, 'Very good. I should reply, "My eyes are fully open to my awful situation." Ruddigore, you know!' He went on, 'You've no idea what it's been like.'

Fortunately, he was right – I did not have any idea what it was like to be accused of theft on a grand scale.

I thought, however, it best not to mention that, but instead said, 'Clive, can you assure me that you have not done anything wrong? It would be far better to come clean at this stage if you have.'

The hands flew up once more. 'How could you even think that? Of course, I haven't done anything wrong.'

I nodded. 'But it's clear from the documents I've been through that the company has paid out £524,252...'

'£524,252 and 83 pence,' Clive corrected me primly.

I paused and looked down at my file. 'Yes, thank you; £524,252 and 83 pence was paid into this false bank account, and that the invoices that purportedly relate to these amounts are forgeries. We have statements from the sub-contractor which clearly show that they have not in fact invoiced you for almost three years.' Clive bowed his head in dumb acceptance. I continued, 'Prima facie, you as financial controller would have the authority to make these payments.'

Clive interrupted. 'Yes, of course. But I don't remember making them, and anyway, all the invoices had the right documentation and were approved by the section managers.'

'But the managers deny that.'

Clive shook his head sadly. 'I know,' he said, 'I suppose that someone forged their signatures as well.'

I pressed on relentlessly, 'Then of course we have the little matter of the Bentley which is apparently sitting in your driveway. How do you afford that on your salary?'

Clive shifted uncomfortably on his seat. 'Well, I...er...I came into a little money.'

'Not £524,252 and 83 pence, by any chance?' I enquired, with more than a hint of irony.

Up went the hands again. 'Really, Ben, please. It was a gift from a dear friend. A *close* friend, if you know what I mean.'

'But we can get confirmation of this from your...er...friend?' I continued.

Clive sighed. 'Yes, I suppose so. If we must.'

'Good.' I went on briskly, 'Well, moving on, if you didn't take the money, who did? Tell me about the other people in the department.'

We discussed at some length Clive's colleagues, and those who had access to records and so on, but came to no very firm conclusion. At the end of our meeting, Clive asked anxiously how it looked.

I again quoted Gilbert & Sullivan, 'Well, we need to add a few things to my report, "merely corroborative detail to give artistic verisimilitude to an otherwise bald and unconvincing narrative".'

Clive looked at me. 'In other words, "here's a pretty mess of things"?'

I could not deny this.

Things stalled for the next few days. Clive's company were at this stage unwilling to call in the police, and so we were unable to approach the bank to investigate the phoney account further. Although, to be honest, any perpetrator worth his salt would have been careful to cover his tracks on that score.

I was mulling over the case one morning and buzzed through to Sue to come to my room. There was no reply for a while, then the phone was answered by Janet.

'Yes?' she barked, in a manner not unlike the crack of a rifle.

'Can you get Sue to come through please, Janet?' I asked.

There was a distinct sniff from the other end of the phone, and I could visualise Janet's lips compressing into a thin line.

'She's not coming in today. Again.' The wave of disapproval was palpable. Janet may have her faults, but I honestly could not remember her ever taking a day off, except for approved holidays.

'Again?' I queried. 'What was the reason?'

Another sniff. I was tempted to enquire solicitously whether Janet had a cold, but decided it would be more prudent to refrain. Janet eventually replied, 'She said something about a slight chill.'

I did not say anything. These absences of Sue's had become more frequent in the last couple of months, and it occurred to me that perhaps she was looking for a new job, and that these days off happened when she had an interview. It would be a pity if she left, I mused, because she was a bright girl, and on a good day, was both efficient and capable. Regrettably, the good days had become fewer and further between recently. However, I did not want to share these thoughts with Janet, who I had observed, did not have much time for Sue.

In a neutral tone, I said, 'OK, Janet, perhaps you could spare me a few minutes from your other work to do a few things for me?'

'I'm on my way,' Janet fired back and the line went dead.

That evening, I was having a relaxing glass or two of Vino Collapso with my old friend Tom Bremner in the local wine bar, Et Alia, which is conveniently located midway between our two offices on the high street. It had proved to be a particularly trying afternoon, as I had been waiting around for some hours at an employment tribunal, ready to give evidence, when at 4:30 pm, the parties had agreed to settle.

'As per!' I complained to Tom, whose client I was representing.

Still, it had been on the whole a satisfactory result as far as we were concerned. 'Added to which,' I went on, 'Sue was off again today, so I had to get Janet to help me prepare this morning.'

I was vaguely aware that Tom was a little *distrait* and kept clearing his throat as if about to impart some vital information. Eventually he said, 'Ben, old chap, I need to say something to you.'

For a second, I thought he was going to put his hand on my knee and declare his undying love. Which would have been all very well, but apart from the fact that I am already spoken for, as it were, Tom is not what you might call a "looker". No, more built for comfort rather than speed, if you get my drift. However, I soon realised that he had other matters on his mind.

He carried on, 'One of our...er...people came to me this morning and said that his "friend" had been browsing online and stumbled across one of those...er...*adult* sites.'

'Adult sites?' I looked blank.

'Yes, adult sites!' Tom sounded impatient. 'You know, they're like dating sites, only they're offering rather more than a cup of coffee in Starbucks.'

Illumination struck. 'You mean a sex site?'

Tom nodded.

'Well, what about it? They're just sites for sad pervs, aren't they? What was your employee's...er..."friend" doing looking there?'

We both knew that there was no such "friend", of course, but Tom ignored that rather disagreeable fact.

'Well, the thing is, Ben, that one of the...er...ladies advertising there looked remarkably like...er...' here Tom gulped 'like your accounts girl, Sue,' he finished in a hurry.

I was stunned into silence for a moment, then laughed out loud. 'Oh, Tom, for a minute you really had me going! It's not April the first, is it?'

'No, no, I'm serious, Ben. The name over the top even says "Sultry Susie",' Tom replied. 'Apparently,' he added quickly.

'Have you seen this...er...advert for yourself?' I asked.

Tom shook his head, albeit not convincingly. I began to have a suspicion that not only was there no "friend", there might not be an employee involved either.

I went on, 'Well, I'd better have a look myself. What's the name of this site? I'll check it out later.'

Tom replied rather self-consciously,

'It's "afternoondelight.com". So I understand.'

We had a couple more glasses of wine, although the atmosphere was a little strained, and I, in particular, was anxious to go and check what I had been told. I hurried the few hundred yards back down the high street to my home and let myself in. The place was in darkness, so it was clear that Marcus, was not home yet. I went into the study, sat down at my desk and stirred the computer into life. I googled afternoondelight.com and clicked on the site.

Perhaps I've led a sheltered life. I was dumbstruck by the sheer number of adverts offering all sorts of activities, and all in a pretty small radius of where I was sitting. I did a search for "Sultry Susie" and there, sure enough was an entry. I quickly clicked on it, and a photograph filled the screen. Although the face was largely covered by a veil of shoulder length hair, there was no doubting it was indeed Sue. She was wearing a sort of loose transparent negligee and kneeling on a bed. Beneath the photograph was a mini-biography, in the form of questions and answers.

My eye was drawn to the question, 'What was your best time ever?' and the hair-raising response, 'In the back of my boss's BMW!'

I gave a snort. Although I do have a BMW, apart from anything else, with my lumbar trouble, there is no way I could manage *that* sort of thing in the back seat.

A bang from the front door announced the arrival of Marcus, and for some reason, feeling strangely guilty, I closed the computer before he put his head round the study door.

'Hi there,' he said, 'What are you up to?'

'Oh, just swotting up a song in case I do another audition.'

'What song is that?'

'Poor wandering hands.'

Marcus looked startled.

'Er, "Poor wandering one", I mean,' I corrected myself hastily.

The next morning I was in early at the office. I had not slept well and such slumber as I managed had been plagued with disturbing dreams.

Never had the words of my favourite Gilbert and Sullivan patter song seemed more apposite:

'When you're lying awake
With a dismal headache
And repose is taboo'd by anxiety...'

What to do about "Sultry Susie"? I decided discreetly to ask my office manager, Janet, what she knew. I learnt that Sue was not married, but did have a long-term boyfriend, Dale. I was tempted to enquire if perhaps he was one of the Yorkshire Dales, but thought better of it, probably wisely. Young Dale was apparently unemployed, or as Janet put it with a sniff, *unemployable*, and things were a bit tight financially. Sue's absences from work had increased in the last two or three months and I asked Janet what reasons Sue had given for this. Janet sniffed and replied that sometimes Sue had just said that she hadn't slept the previous night and was exhausted.

If she was engaged in the activities she was advertising, this was not surprising, I thought wryly. I instructed Janet to contact the wayward Sue and find out when she proposed to return.

Putting the matter to one side, I turned my attention to the report I was preparing, again another client of Tom's. It was a rather depressing case, concerning a single mother who had been accused of benefit fraud. The girl in question had been employed in a pub, more or less full time, but had told the benefits agency that she only worked twelve hours a week, so that she could claim additional benefits. Although she was clearly guilty of this, I could not help having sympathy for her. She was admittedly somewhat on the rough side, and had no educational qualifications, but she was trying to do her best to provide for herself and her six-year-old in difficult circumstances. Still, the gravity of the offence meant that, according to Tom, she was facing a custodial sentence. My task was to provide a report challenging the Benefits Agency's estimate of the scale of the "theft", which they put at some £50,000 or so.

To add to the pressure, this was a legal-aid case, so my fees were restricted, to put it mildly. Faced with the dilemma of doing what I thought was right, and what was profitable, I knew that I would err on the side of the former, which would mean effectively putting in some hours of unpaid time.

The words of the Pirate King in *The Pirates of Penzance* came to mind: "Always act in accordance with the dictates of your conscience, my boy, and chance the consequences."

Sometimes I curse my conscience…

Janet poked her head around my door later in the afternoon, with an envelope in her hand. Sue had been signed off by her doctor for a fortnight, suffering from stress, but she had, rather oddly, offered to come in after normal office hours if there was something in particular that I wanted her to do. I pondered the significance of this offer. A thought struck me: Sue still had keys to the office and the codes for the alarm system. Perhaps she was using the office as a venue to entertain her clients. I shuddered, with hideous visions of frantic coupling on the boardroom table's highly polished surface. It was all I could do to refrain from rushing to inspect its surface for any tell-tale scratches.

Pulling myself together, I asked Janet to call Sue to take her up on this offer, and arrange a suitable time.

'And, Janet,' I added, 'I think it would be as well if you were here too.' Janet looked at me quizzically, and so I felt obliged to tell her the whole story.

Janet listened in silence, her lips gradually pursing tighter and tighter. I have mentioned that she is also a fellow member of CAOS (the County Amateur Operatic Society) and enthusiast of the Savoy Operas. She is somewhat typecast by her physical appearance but she had a minor triumph as Katisha in *The Mikado* some years ago. As a character, Katisha is probably the most interesting of all the Gilbert and Sullivan contralto roles, certainly one of the most demanding both vocally and artistically. The tricky part of the role is to get the audience to hate this awful old bag who comes between the young lovers but later to reveal a soft and vulnerable side and ultimately gain its sympathy. In point of fact, I had yet to discover Janet's soft side, but there was no doubting her diligence and ruthless efficiency. She would, I thought, be an admirable chaperone for me in what promised to be a delicate interview.

Janet duly made the call, and an arrangement was made for the following day at 6 pm, after the other staff would be gone. Janet advised me of this and asked how I was looking forward to it.

In an attempt to lighten the mood, I quoted some *Iolanthe*:

'*Every journey has an end –*
When at the worst affairs will mend –
Dark the dawn when day is nigh –
Hustle your horse and don't say die!'

Janet's expression didn't flicker, but she replied, 'Here's some more *Iolanthe* for you then:

'*I heard the minx remark,*
She'd meet him after dark,
Inside St James's Park,
And give him one!'

It was the nearest I'd ever heard her get to humour.

I stayed late that evening at the office to complete the report on the Benefits Agency case, then strolled down the high street to my home. Marcus was sprawled on the sofa watching TV in the little sitting area just off the kitchen.

'What's for dinner?' I asked.

Marcus grunted and replied shortly, 'I've already eaten.'

The empty packet of an Indian ready-meal which had once contained the last mortal remains of some factory-fed chicken bore testimony to this remark.

'You might have left some for me!' I protested, 'I've been cooking the books all day so I don't want to be cooking now!'

This admittedly somewhat flimsy attempt at the jocular fell on stony ears, and there was a resounding silence.

Marcus suddenly said, 'Anyway, I thought you'd be too busy with your other activities to be bothered to eat here. I'm off to bed!'

And with that cryptic remark, he leapt up and exited the room with a slam of the door. I am supposedly the one in the household with a thespian inclination, but Marcus at times has an undoubted histrionic bent.

Marcus was due to fly to Budapest early in the morning, but declined my offer of a lift to the airport and left without a farewell, leaving me wondering in what way I had offended him. It just seemed one more of life's little tribulations…

The following day seemed to drag wearily by, but eventually 6 pm approached. Sure enough, at a few minutes before, Janet buzzed me to say, 'She's here. And she's come with the "boyfriend".'

This was a bit of a surprise. Why was Sue's boyfriend here?

'OK,' I replied, 'You'd better sit him in reception with a cup of coffee, then come into my room with Sue.'

I certainly didn't want to say what I had to with Dale there as well. Sue entered my office, followed by Janet, who firmly shut the door and then busied herself by pretending to file papers.

I stood up at their entry and motioned Sue to a chair on the other side of my desk. I looked closely at her. I think I expected some transformation into a sultry seductive siren, but in fact she just looked ordinary. She was wearing a red jacket with the collar turned up against the cold, and a matching peaked cap pulled down over her eyes. The whole effect was somewhat reminiscent of a letter box. I had not entirely prepared what I was going to say.

My first reaction on seeing Sue on the website afternoondelight.com was to fire her immediately. I had rung one of Tom's partners, who specialises in employment law, to ask his advice.

Rather to my surprise, he had told me to act cautiously.

'If you went for instant dismissal it's possible she might go to an employment tribunal,' he had said.

'So?' I had replied, 'Surely they would find in my firm's favour?'

'Well, not necessarily,' he had warned, 'and there could be unwelcome publicity.'

'Yes, but she wouldn't want that,' I argued.

'Neither would you,' he had pointed out, reasonably. 'And of course, unfair dismissal has the potential for unlimited damages…'

That line had struck home. The words of my illustrious namesake, Ben Jonson, are sometimes quoted at me. Marcus knows his drama and if I am being in a particularly thrifty mood, will quote the opening lines of *Volpone*:

'Good morning to the day, and next, my gold…'

These thoughts were whirling around my brain as I too sat down. There was a slight pause as I mentally girded my loins (an unfortunate choice of phrase in the circumstances perhaps) and struck out into deep water, as it were.

'Good of you to come in, Sue,' I started. I was trying hard not to make this sound ironic. I'm not sure I succeeded, for Sue looked at me uncertainly. I carried on, 'How are you?'

She mumbled something incoherent.

'Your sick note says you're suffering from stress,' I said, 'I hope it's nothing we've done?'

If I was expecting a firm rebuttal, I was disappointed. My mind was still on the unlimited damages…

'Well, it's everything really,' she said. She looked me full in the face, her long hair falling down to her shoulders now that it had been released from the confines of the cap.

For a few minutes we talked about her health problems and the difficulties she was having with her accounting studies. I finally became aware that Janet was banging filing cabinet drawers with unnecessary force and glaring at me behind Sue's back. I fixed her with a steely look then concentrated on the matter in hand.

As casually as I could I said, 'Sue, if I said afternoondelight.com to you, what would you say?'

Sue's mouth hung open in shock, and the colour drained from her cheeks like the tide from the beach. If I had any doubts as to the identity of "Sultry Susie", they were completely dispelled.

'It is you, isn't it?' I asked.

She nodded in dumb acceptance.

'Well,' I said, 'a number of points arise then, don't they?' I started to feel as though I were addressing a shareholders' meeting.

'Firstly,' I went on, 'this…er…matter was brought to my attention by someone outside the firm. So you are potentially bringing this firm into disrepute. As we are a respected, not to say, respectable business,' I was warming to my theme now, 'this is a matter of some concern.'

'Secondly, there is the subject of your health and safety. I see from your…er…advert that you do what I believe are known as "outcalls". That means that you go to the, shall we say, *punters'*, address or an hotel or something?'

Sue nodded once more.

'Well. You can see how dangerous that could be, surely? And of course, there is the risk of…er…infections and so on.' I felt that I could not look at her anymore, so stood up and started to pace the floor. Janet meanwhile was in a state of paralysis, her hand hovering in mid-air, clutching a sheaf of papers, and with an expression of horrified fascination, like an onlooker to a car crash.

'Thirdly, does your boyfriend – Dale, isn't it – know what you are doing?' I gave a brief glance in Sue's direction and saw that she was nodding.

'Hmm,' I said, then continued in my most portentous manner, 'Well, then, he could be construed to be living on immoral earnings!'

Sue looked at me questioningly.

'That means he could be prosecuted by the police if they find out,' I explained.

She seemed even further stunned by this.

'And fourthly – and perhaps most importantly,' I said pompously, 'Have you declared your earnings to the Inland Revenue? We are a firm of accountants, you know, and we have a duty to ensure these matters are dealt with properly.' I could not resist adding, 'As they say in *The Pirates of Penzance*,

"Oh, is there not one maiden breast,
Which does not feel the moral beauty?" '

Janet's lips tightened into a thin line at this. It suddenly occurred to me that talk of maiden's breasts was perhaps not the happiest topic in the circumstances. There were a few further minutes of somewhat stilted conversation after that, which concluded with Sue agreeing that she would cease her activities and forthwith take down her entry from the website. She seemed to have forgotten that she was there ostensibly to do some work, and was anxious to escape, as indeed was I.

She left the room and Janet escorted her, together with Dale, from the building. Janet returned to my office after a couple of minutes.

'Well, I think that went quite well, didn't it?' I said brightly.

'Did it?' Janet looked grim.

'Oh, I think so,' I went on, 'she's agreed to stop all that sort of carry-on, and says she'll be back at work in a couple of weeks.'

'And you believed her?' Janet sounded sceptical.

'Yes, I did. I think I talked some sense into her,' I replied, a little nettled at Janet's attitude.

Janet gave a sardonic smile. 'Well, to quote further from *The Pirates of Penzance*,

"Oh, false one. You have deceived me!" '

'We'll see!' I retorted, stung by her riposte.

'Indeed we will!' Janet said over her shoulder as she left the room.

Over the next few days, I checked the website afternoondelight.com each evening when I got home – I did not want to do so at the office in case somehow other members of staff found the link. I was pleased that after a couple of days, "Sultry Susie" was no longer displaying her charms, so to speak.

I relayed this information to Janet who looked dubious, but I said to her in my most supercilious tone, 'You really ought to have more faith in people, Janet. I knew Sue would see sense after our little chat. She's really not that sort of girl.' Janet didn't reply, but flashed me one of her gimlet looks, which left me feeling uncomfortable.

'She's not that sort of girl,' I repeated stubbornly to Janet's retreating back.

I tried to put all this to the back of my mind and turned once more to the case of Clive Pettit and the disappearing money. I had spoken again to the CEO of Strand Electrics, but he was still dragging his feet about calling in the police. Something had to be done, I decided, although at present, I was not entirely sure what that should be.

I was still turning this problem over in my mind that evening, sitting at the kitchen table, waiting for Marcus to reappear. There was a slight froideur in the atmosphere as he had again been in Budapest, though he was cagey about the job he was working on. He finally arrived home and went straight to the fridge.

'I'm starving,' he announced, retrieving a banana from behind some cans of lager.

'Is there anything to put on this?' he asked, 'You know, that stuff that pretends to be cream, but isn't.'

Some lines from *H.M.S Pinafore* sprang to my mind:
'Things are seldom what they seem,
Skim milk masquerades as cream,
Black sheep dwell in every fold,
All that glitters is not gold.'

I hummed, passing a carton to Marcus. Then I suddenly stopped. Something rang a bell at the back of my mind. What was it? Something in the chorus I had just been humming. I involuntarily let go of the carton, which, fortunately, Marcus caught just in time before it hit the floor. He called after me in puzzlement as I ran from the room and went to the study to look at my papers on the Pettit case.

I thumbed quickly through the files, then retrieved the notes of my interview with Clive. Yes, there it was. That was the answer. Now, all I had to do was prove it…

First thing the next morning, I rang Clive and put some questions to him. His answers confirmed my thoughts. Janet, who had been hovering around my desk during the call, attempting to get my signature on some invoices, looked at me quizzically.

'What was all that about?' she asked.

'I'll tell you later,' I said and grabbing my jacket, hurried off out of the office.

Some twenty minutes later, I swung into the car park in front of Strand Electrics. I climbed out and strode into the reception area.

'Could I have a word with the CEO, please?' I asked the girl behind the desk. She had a curvaceous figure and a mass of auburn hair tumbling on to her shoulders. "All out of a bottle!" I could almost hear my mother sniffing in disapproval.

She reached for the phone, 'I'll just see if he's in. Who should I say it is?'

'The name's Jonson, Ben Jonson,' I replied.

I noticed her hand pause momentarily, as if she recognised my name, but she punched in a number. She half turned, so that I had difficulty hearing the conversation. She replaced the receiver then swung back to face me.

'He's just with someone at the moment. Would you mind waiting a few minutes? Can I get you a coffee?'

I declined the offer of drink, and was about to sit down, when I had another thought. Muttering some excuse about having forgotten something, I went back to my car and slumped down in the driver's seat. I did not have to wait long. From the side entrance, a figure emerged and scurried towards a grey Mercedes. Before he had a chance to open the door, I was out of the car and sprinted the few yards across the tarmac.

'Nearly missed you!' I exclaimed breezily, sticking out a hand, 'The name's Jonson.'

The man hesitated a second, then muttered, 'Yes, I was just…er…getting something from the car.'

'Go ahead,' I replied.

'Oh, it doesn't matter now. You'd better come to my office.'

He turned and I followed him back into the building. He paused as he passed the receptionist.

'It's OK, Janice,' he murmured to her then carried on.

We walked down a long corridor, then eventually reached a door marked "David Gold – CEO" which he opened and we went in. 'You'd better sit down,' he said then realising this sounded ungracious, corrected himself. 'I mean, please take a seat, Mr Jonson.'

'Call me Ben,' I said, still maintaining a bright tone.

There was a pause. 'I suppose this is about Clive and the…er…defalcations?' he began.

'Of course,' I responded.

There was another pause.

'Er…you've been hired by Clive to try to help him, I believe,' Gold went on.

I nodded in affirmation. 'And how is it going?' Gold asked, clearing his throat.

'Oh, I think rather well. Certainly as far as Clive is concerned.'

He looked somewhat nonplussed at this, but said, 'That's good.'

'Isn't it?' I responded enthusiastically, 'Well, at least it's good for Clive. Not so good for you, though.'

There was a pause. 'What do you mean?' he asked, his face draining of colour.

'Oh, I think you know what I mean, don't you?' I said.

He looked me in the eyes for some moments. I held his gaze until eventually he looked away. 'You haven't got any proof,' he said finally.

'Well, at the moment, circumstantial proof only, I have to admit,' I replied, still maintaining the breezy tone, 'but we will find other evidence I'm sure.'

Gold sat dumbly in his seat.

'Yes,' I went on, 'I expect we will find it in the end. Probably a dummy account to which you could transfer cash, then take it out bit by bit, so that no one would notice. An overseas account, so that your accountants would be more easily fooled, I would hazard.'

Gold sat silently, ashen-faced.

'How did it start?' I asked, but then went on quickly, 'No, don't tell me, let me guess. You probably needed a slug of money quickly for some reason – what was it? House purchase? Race-horse? Hot tip on the stock-market? Whatever it was, you saw a way of taking the money without anyone noticing, and you said to yourself "I'll pay it back next week, or next month, when the money from the sale of the house, or the sale of the shares, or the sale of the horse, comes in". And possibly you did pay it back. That time. But then you got to thinking "that was easy. I can do it again". And you did. Perhaps you did it a few times. And then you realised that nobody noticed. And so you didn't bother to pay it back. And you took some more – probably a flutter on the stock-market? But then the share price fell. And then you couldn't pay it back, even if you had wanted to. How am I doing?'

Gold looked stunned. 'How did you know all that?' he asked.

'Because I've seen it all before. Too many times,' I replied briskly.

'What are you going to do?' Gold said.

'I'm not really going to anything. But you are,' I said. 'Firstly, you are going to reinstate Clive and make it clear that he's not implicated in all this.'

Gold nodded.

'Then you need to talk to your fellow directors and shareholders. I took the liberty of checking with Companies House, so I know you aren't the major shareholder. It's up to them what they do. Strictly speaking, I probably should report all this to the relevant authorities, but provided you do what I say, I'll stay out of it. At least for the time being.'

Gold nodded once again in acquiescence. I stood up and went to the door.

'Oh, one more thing,' I said, 'if I were you, I would stop the fling with the lovely Janice straightaway. You're going to need all the help you can get from your wife right now.'

Once more, Gold looked stunned. 'How did you know...?'

I tapped the side of my nose. 'I have a scent for these things,' I said in my most conspiratorial manner and swept out of the room.

Really, I thought to myself, *the G&S thing is giving me a distinct flair for the dramatic!*

I called in on Clive Pettit to give him the good news that he was in the clear. He was close to tears and made as if to embrace me, but stopped himself just in time, to my great relief.

'But how did you find out it was David?'

'Well, it was a piece from *H.M.S Pinafore* that got me thinking – you know, that line "All that glitters is not gold". It reminded me that the CEO was called Gold.'

'It must have been more than that?'

'Well, it was a start. And that's why I rang you and asked those questions.'

'Such as "Did David never take holiday", "Did he come in early and stay late" and "What is his background?"'

Clive looked at me with his plump head on one side.

'Yes, that's right. When you replied "yes" to the first two questions, I was fairly sure. It's a typical sign of someone who's on the fiddle that they want to be around all the time. Then when you said he had been an accountant originally, that made me even more certain. He had the opportunity and the expertise to take the money, and because of his position, he would probably be able to stop you from asking too many questions.'

'And how did you know about Janice?'

I grinned. 'Oh, a lucky guess really. But again, experience has taught me that very often someone like Gold is having a bit of extra-marital with a girl from the office. Then the way she spoke to him on the phone, and the way he stopped by her desk, made it pretty obvious.'

'Was she involved in it?'

I frowned. 'That I don't know for certain. My guess is that she was, to some extent – Gold probably got her.to do things for him which she must have known weren't proper. But it's possible she didn't know all the ins and outs. And it is almost certain that she will deny everything.'

Clive looked tearful again. 'Oh, Ben, what can I say? How can I repay you?'

I thought to myself that he would see soon enough when I rendered my fee note, but then a thought struck me.

'Well, actually, Clive, I was a little disappointed at the audition the other day...'

Clive's eyes narrowed and he gave a little snort. 'Hmph! *"Faint heart never won fair lady"* eh?'

I grinned, though thinking it was stretching credibility to describe Clive as a "fair lady".

'You see, Clive, I thought perhaps you could have a new take on "Patience" – something more muscular? After all, Bunthorne is only *pretending* to be an aesthete, isn't he?'

Clive pulled a face. 'Possibly so, my dear Ben. The only snag is, we're not doing "Patience" now. We've decided to do *Pirates* instead.' He obviously saw my expression, as he put a hand up and went on, 'But I take your point, and I'll see what I can do.'

Meanwhile, I had passed my report about the benefits "fraud" to Tom.

One morning, he rang in some excitement.

'Are you sure you're right about this, Ben?' he started.

'Yes, I believe so,' I replied.

'Blood and sand!' he exclaimed – Tom has an unusual line in expletives – 'I'll get on to the CPS straightaway!'

The conclusion of my report had been somewhat surprising. Although we had to concede the Benefits Agency claim that Tom's client had lied about the number of hours she worked, I had discovered that she was in fact entitled to, but had not claimed, two other benefits instead. As a result, I concluded, that had she claimed correctly, not only would she not *owe* the government £50,000, they would owe *her* about £5,000. So although technically guilty of fraud, I hoped that in the circumstances, common sense would prevail.

I fell into a reverie contrasting this affair with that of Sue. The one girl trying to make ends meet by working hard in a pub, bringing up a child on her own with no support, and the other seeing an easy way to make money. From a purely legal point of view, it was the former who had broken the law, yet from every other aspect, it seemed to me to be Sue who was the guilty party. Although the "Sultry Susie" tale undoubtedly had its funny side, I recalled that when face to face with the real person behind that persona, to think of the things she actually did with the "punters" made me feel distinctly uncomfortable, not to say profoundly sad.

The phone buzzed and Janet came through, reminding me of the rehearsal for the forthcoming production of *Pirates*. Clive had been as good as his word. By a stroke of good luck, he had been too preoccupied with his own problems to get around to finalising the casting for the operetta, but as soon as he had received the "all clear" from me, had done so. I had landed the part of Frederic, and although this had ruffled a few feathers with some of the older hands, Clive had managed to smooth things over with vague promises of greater glories to come in subsequent productions.

The rehearsal did not go as well as I had expected. Perhaps I had pushed my luck as far as Clive was concerned, because after my first song he had stopped proceedings and said in a cutting tone, 'Yes, Ben, dear, I realise it is difficult in your first major part. Frederic's part is written for a tenor though, which I know you are…' there was a pause, 'on your day.'

For a heart-stopping moment, I thought he was going to recast me, but he went on in a more emollient tone to suggest ways of improving my delivery.

Not so fortunate was "Mabel", who kept getting her lines wrong. Clive lost his cool and after yet another intemperate outburst from our director, poor "Mabel" burst into tears and cried, 'I can't understand it. I knew my lines backward yesterday.'

'And that's how you're saying them, dear!' replied Clive, with some asperity.

I was relieved when we finally finished for the evening and as we trooped out, I whispered to Janet, 'I'm going for a drink,' and made my escape to Et Alia, where I had an urgent appointment with a bottle of chardonnay.

As I entered the wine bar, I espied my old chum and source of lucrative work, Tom Bremner, sitting in one corner. I took over my bottle and glass, and plonked myself down next to him.

'Mind if I join you?' I enquired.

'Ah, Ben,' he said, 'of course!'

'In fact,' he continued, 'I'm glad you came in. I was going to call you in the morning.'

'Oh, have you spoken to the CPS?' I asked.

'The CPS?' He looked a bit at sea.

'About the benefit fraud case,' I prompted.

'What? Oh yes, I did. Actually,' he lowered his voice, 'I have good news about that. The CPS have read your report and indicated that they are going to drop all charges.'

'Well, that's good news,' I said.

'Yes, well done to you,' Tom beamed at me. 'Of course, that's not official yet – we will probably have to go for a meeting with the judge in Chambers, but I have high hopes!' He clinked his glass against mine, and took a hefty swig of wine. He went on, 'But it was about another little matter that I wanted to speak to you.'

He looked slightly shifty as he spoke, and I began to get a sinking feeling in my stomach. 'Yes,' he cleared his throat, 'You know I spoke to you the other week about your accounts girl...'

The sinking feeling accelerated into a crash dive as I nodded.

'Well, I notice...er...my employee's *friend* has noticed – that "Sultry Susie" is no longer on that site.'

'No,' I replied feeling relieved, 'I had a firm word with her and I think that's all sorted out now.'

'Yes, well, I wouldn't be too sure about that!' said Tom. 'If I were you, I'd look again.'

I groaned. 'Oh, God, no!' I said, 'What is she now? "Sexy Sue" I suppose?'

Tom, shook his head. 'No,' he said, 'try "D-Cup Debbie!"'

I reeled under the shock of Tom's revelation. Not least of my concerns was the image of Janet the next morning giving me one of her piercing looks with "I told you so" writ large across her visage. After leaving Tom, I hurried home and checked the site afternoondelight.com for myself. Sure enough, there was a photograph of Sue with the heading "D-Cup Debbie".

As if to add verisimilitude to this eye-catching by-line, the photograph showed her leaning forwards to reveal a cleft of cleavage the size of the Grand Canyon, and her face heavily made up with grotesquely rose-bud lips and deep eye-shadow.

The next day, when I reached my office I instructed Janet to get hold of Sue, and ignoring the words of advice of the solicitor, threw caution aside and told Sue in no uncertain terms that her immediate resignation, with a month's salary in lieu, would oblige. Janet, who had been standing opposite me whilst I made the call, nodded her head in approval.

'That's the stuff to give her!' she said, and her lips smacked in relish.

Having wound myself up into a state of righteous indignation, I could only agree, though I have to confess to being mightily relieved when I received Sue's acknowledgement of her waiver of all claims against my firm the next day. There is definitely something of the Volpone in me...

When I got home that evening, I found Marcus back from Brussels and sitting at my desk in the study. I greeted him effusively, but he shook off my efforts at a warm embrace.

'Save all that for your other conquests!' he cried.

I looked at him uncomprehendingly for a second, then he angrily swung the computer screen round to face me. There, leering out from the screen was "D-Cup Debbie".

All then fell into place: Marcus's coolness had all arisen from the fact that I had carelessly forgotten to close my computer down and he had discovered I had been looking at the afternoondelight.com site.

Ignoring my immediate reaction to be annoyed with him for doubting my fidelity, I rapidly explained all that had gone on. When I had finished, he looked abashed, and moisture filled his eyes.

'I'm sorry,' he stammered, 'it's just that I...' he didn't seem able to find the words to explain. Privately, I thought that it was the possibility that I had been with women that upset him more that the act of infidelity itself...

He gave me a hug, and as he pulled away, he tried to grin through his tears. Somehow, he looked different, though I couldn't quite put my finger on why. Then something clicked.

'So how was the dentist in Budapest?' I asked.

Marcus looked surprised for a moment. 'You guessed! I thought you wouldn't notice!'

'I'm not totally unobservant,' I retorted, 'So that explains all the secretive trips to Hungary?'

Marcus looked sheepish. 'I thought you might not approve of the expense, but it's a lot cheaper over there.'

'You really are a prize chump sometimes, you know,' I said lightly, 'Come, as G&S put it in *Pirates*, "Oh dry the glistening tear that dews that martial cheek!"'

2. Ben Jonson and a Day
at the Races

I was in my office one morning disconsolately staring at the local paper when Janet, my Rottweiler of an office manager, hove into view. I tried to conceal my reading matter, whilst simultaneously cursing the "open door" policy that is de rigueur these days.

I was unsuccessful in my attempts, as Janet, with her eagle eye, said, 'Oh! I see you've been reading the review of *Pirates* in The Clarion.'

A denial was useless in the face of this merciless raptor of the admin department. 'I did just glance at it,' I replied, in what I hoped would pass for a casual manner.

It was the day after our third performance of *The Pirates of Penzance*, put on in the town's "Little Theatre" by CAOS, that is, the County Amateur Operatic Society, of which Janet was a stalwart member, and I an enthusiastic newcomer.

After some unexpected twists and turns, I had auditioned for a part in *Pirates* and been cast as Frederic, a slight disappointment as far as I was concerned, since I had fancied performing the "patter" song, "I am the very model of a modern major general", which of course is sung by the eponymous Major-General Stanley.

However, in true thespian tradition, I had given the role my all, and felt I had turned in a creditable performance. Not so, according to the reporter for The Clarion. Janet, who had appeared in the role of Ruth, a "Piratical Maid of all work" according to the programme, a veritable triumph of type-casting, especially as regards the "Piratical" aspect, picked up the paper and started to read out loud:

'Last night's performance of The Pirates of Penzance *was very much a curate's egg affair. On the one hand, Janet Mathieson, as "Ruth" stole the show with her rendition of "When Fredric was a little lad".*

On the other, Frederic himself, in the person of local accountant Ben Jonson was so mind-numbingly wooden that he should be classified as a fire risk. Perhaps the director (the businessman Clive Pettit) should tell Mr Jonson that simply being on a stage doesn't make you an actor, any more than standing in a garage makes you a car...'

I tried snatching the offending periodical out of Janet's hand, but she nimbly sidestepped me and continued,

'He would be lucky to get a gig directing traffic...he stopped the show, but then the show wasn't travelling very fast at the time...'

I finally pulled the paper out of Janet's hands and thrust it in the bin.

'Oh, dear,' she said, trying hard to conceal a huge grin, and failing dismally, 'that was a bit harsh.'

'Yes, it was,' I replied somewhat shortly, 'and you haven't got to the part where he says "As for his singing voice, he ought to be arrested for being in possession of an offensive weapon." Anyway, enough of that, did you want me?'

'Oh, yes,' Janet said, 'I was nearly forgetting. Tom Bremner called whilst you were away from your desk and asked if you wanted to go to the races with him this afternoon.'

'The races?' I said in some astonishment, 'I didn't think Tom was a racing man!'

Janet pursed her lips. 'No he is not, and quite right too! I don't approve of all that sort of carry-on.' Janet's strict non-conformist upbringing was coming to the fore, I thought.

She went on, 'No, the thing is, Tom's had an invitation for two people to go to the races, but his usual companion has let him down at the last minute, so he wondered if you would like to come instead.'

I thought about this for a second, mulling over the slight irritation at only being on the "B" list of invitees, as it were.

But my diary was fairly clear, it was a bright sunny day, so I nodded and said to Janet, 'OK, ring him back, please, and say yes. And find out the arrangements,' I added as Janet sailed majestically out of the room.

Tom Bremner, as I have mentioned before, is a solicitor friend and drinking companion of mine who has a practice further along the high street from my office, and we frequently meet at the end of the day in our local wine bar, Et Alia, to review the day's events and drown our sorrows or celebrate, as the case may be. Tom is a frequent (and profitable) source of clients for my firm, and though normally, the referrals are to do with divorce cases, or accident or compensation claims, from time to time, something of a more substantial nature comes my way, such as the case of Clive Pettit, my erstwhile director in *Pirates*, who was accused of misappropriation of funds on a grand scale from his employer.

With a little perseverance and studying of the data, I had managed to clear his good name and find the real culprit. For this, he felt he owed me a debt of gratitude, and that is why I managed to get a role in the production of *Pirates*. But after such excoriating reviews from the press, in the form of The Clarion, perhaps the well of his gratitude might begin to run dry. I would have to take steps...

At precisely midday, Tom's Mercedes pulled up outside my office, and I was ushered into the rear seat where Tom himself was ensconced.

'I've got my assistant, Roddy, to drop us off. He'll come and get us when we're ready, so we don't have to worry about having a drink or two, eh?'

'Oh, good,' I replied, 'Thank you very much, Roddy.'

'My pleasure,' said the obliging Roddy, as he simultaneously engaged "drive" and floored the throttle. With a yelp from the tyres, the Merc rocketed up the high street, and Tom and I were thrust back in our seats by the sudden force.

'Steady on, Roddy,' cried Tom, 'I'd quite like to get this car back in one piece later!'

Roddy grinned and the car slowed. 'Sorry, Tom,' he said, 'I'm not used to driving something this powerful. My usual mode of transport is a ten-year-old Fiesta.'

Tom looked as though he was about to say something cutting, so in an attempt to smooth matters, I quickly enquired, 'Who is our benefactor today, Tom? I take it that someone else is paying?'

'Of course,' he said with a smile, 'I wouldn't waste my money on it! Actually, our host is a rival of yours, Ben. Keith Huxley of Huxley and Co.'

'Ah!' I replied, and fell silent.

Huxley and Co was a firm in a neighbouring market town, and Keith and I had crossed swords, so to speak, on a number of occasions. We had each attracted clients from the other, though I thought without undue hubris that I had been on the winning end of that particular tug-of-war. The firm had been founded by Keith and I had to admit to a certain jealousy that Keith had built it up fairly rapidly and successfully so that it was now a substantial practice.

Tom interrupted my thoughts by outlining the programme for the day. 'First, we have a drink or two in the "Hampstead Suite", then a sit-down lunch, then there are a couple of private boxes we can use to watch the gee-gees afterwards.'

'Sounds like hard work!' I responded.

'Well, someone's got to do it!' Tom said with a grin.

Twenty minutes later, we were deposited by Roddy at the entrance to the main stand, and he roared off once more.

'I'll have his guts for garters if he damages that car!' said Tom grimly, as he watched the Mercedes disappear into the traffic.

We were ushered into the "Hampstead Suite" by a uniformed flunkey, and a glass of slightly tepid champagne was thrust into our hands. Tom, being the sociable sort he is, soon surrounded us with a crowd of friends, acquaintances and business contacts, and I found myself standing next to the father of one of my son Sam's school friends, a chap called Nicholas Emmett.

'Ah, Ben,' he cried, 'how good to see you. It's been quite a while.'

I agreed it had.

'I was just thinking of you earlier when I was reading The Clarion and the review of *The Pirates of Penzance* and…Oh dear,' he stumbled, obviously recalling just what The Clarion had said about me.

'Still, all publicity is good publicity, or something like that,' he went on quickly.

I could feel myself colouring but tried to adopt an air of insouciance and said, 'Oh yes? I haven't had time to glance at the paper as yet.'

He held my gaze for a moment or two as if trying to decide whether this was true or not, but finally decided to give me the benefit of the doubt and nodded.

'Funnily enough, my wife pointed out that the review was written by none other than the son of our esteemed host today, Keith Huxley. I hadn't noticed that.'

Momentarily intrigued, I said, 'No, I hadn't noticed that either,' before realising that I was supposed not to have seen the offending piece. Fortunately, Nicholas was already speaking and appeared not to hear.

'In fact, Ben, I was also thinking about you for another reason. More in a professional way, actually.'

I felt that twitch in the stomach which I always get when I sense some remunerative work coming my way.

'Yes,' Nicholas continued, 'you know, I was so impressed with the way you conducted yourself after the…' he paused, searching for the right phrase, 'after the *passing* of your wife that I really wanted to put our affairs your way. But you know how it is.'

I assured him that I did, though without actually any clear idea of what he meant.

'But the way things are, I'm not happy,' Nicholas went on, 'not happy at all. Do you have a card?' he asked suddenly, and I automatically reached in my pocket and produced one.

Unfortunately, our host, Keith Huxley shimmied up to us just as I was handing the card over.

'Ah, naughty, naughty!' he cried in a pseudo-playful way, 'You shouldn't come here just to poach my best clients, Ben!'

Feeling somewhat embarrassed, I muttered something about Nicholas being interested in joining the Operatic Society which was why I was passing him my number. Although Nicholas nodded in affirmation, I could tell Keith was not convinced and he said,

'I'm surprised you would want to carry on with that Ben, after the review in The Clarion.'

This was a bit of a nasty one, but Nicholas interrupted before I could think of a reply.

'Oh, Ben hasn't seen the paper yet,' he said, 'Apparently.'

'A treat in store for you then, Ben,' Keith replied coolly, before moving off to another group.

Nicholas too moved away with a brief 'I'll be in touch' and I was left alone for a moment, before a familiar voice said from behind me, 'Didn't expect you to show your face in public today!'

It was Clive Pettit, our director of the operatic society, not normally my favourite person I have to say, but I was quite relieved to see a friendly face, so to speak, after the little run-in with Keith. I gave a wry smile. 'Not quite what I had hoped for in The Clarion I have to admit, Clive.'

'Well, I thought they were quite unfair, dear boy,' Clive responded, much to my surprise, 'and in any case, I know that the reporter sloped off after only about twenty minutes.'

I raised my eyebrows in query.

'Oh, I always keep tabs on the press, my darling,' Clive said as his hands flew up in his characteristic gesture. 'You know, find them the best seats, ply them with a few G&Ts beforehand and in the interval, and watch them during the performance. Usually works well – the lad from the Evening Echo was well away by the end and gave us a lovely little piece the other night.'

I made a mental note to track down a copy of the Echo to try to salvage my wounded pride.

'Anyway,' Clive went on, 'I don't know why the reporter from The Clarion seemed to have it in for you. Have you upset him in some way?'

'Not that I know of,' I replied, 'though someone just mentioned that he is apparently the son of our host, Keith Huxley.'

'Oh, well then,' Clive said, enigmatically, 'but he was wrong about you. You're not *that* wooden.'

'Thanks very much, Clive,' I responded, dryly. 'That makes me feel a lot better. Changing the subject, what are you doing here?'

'Well, that's a good question. Usually, of course, it's only board members who get asked to these "dos", but since the CEO has left, as you know only too well, my dear Ben, then I got the short straw. Keith Huxley's firm are our auditors, you see,' he added, by way of explanation. 'It's not really my thing, you know,' he went on in a confidential tone, 'I'd much rather be getting on with *The Gondoliers*.'

This was to be the next production by CAOS. In a bid to restore my somewhat tarnished reputation and improve my chances at the auditions, I quickly burst into song,

'My papa, he keeps three horses,
Black, and white, and dapple grey, sir;
Turn three times, then take your courses,
Catch whichever girl you may, sir!'

Clive gave a somewhat mirthless smile and said, 'Oh, yes, *The Gondoliers* themselves, very good, Ben. Quite appropriate for the races, of course. Though,' he added, 'I'm not sure you and I will be catching many girls, eh?'

And with that, he sashayed off into the crowd.

Just then, a bell sounded and we were summoned to lunch. I found myself on a table sitting opposite Tom and alongside Nicholas Emmett, with a bunch of Tom's cronies, who were obviously intent on having a good time.

Nicholas turned to me and said, 'As I was saying, I'm not happy at all.'

'In what way?' I asked, 'Do you mean with the fees?'

'Well, yes, the fees are terribly high,' replied Nicholas, 'though having said that, I wouldn't *mind* that too much in itself, as long as I was getting a decent service.'

'And you're not?'

'Not really,' Nicholas said, pausing for a moment as he was served a rather lurid looking prawn cocktail, 'I mean, I don't mind so much paying through the nose if I get Keith's personal attention to stuff, but usually I have to deal with his sidekick, a rather creepy young man, Douglas something-or-other, who always seems a bit evasive, if you know what I mean.'

'Can you be a bit more specific?'

'Well, for instance, you may know that there's a trust fund which pays the school and university fees for my kids, and Keith is a trustee, so he organises all the payments and so on. But I keep getting reminders from the school that the fees are outstanding, so I chase it up, and this Douglas fobs me off with some excuse or other, such as "we're waiting for some funds to come off deposit" or "the brokers need to raise some funds but they're waiting until the stock goes ex-div" or some such. Not that I really understand what he's on about. What is "ex div" anyway?'

I opened my mouth to explain but was interrupted by the arrival of my prawn cocktail, and before I could continue, Nicholas was off again.

'Well, it doesn't really matter – I probably wouldn't understand the explanation anyway. The point is, I think this Doug is not being straight with me.'

'But are the fees paid in the end?' I asked, as a nagging suspicion crossed my mind.

'Oh, yes, they are. In the end. It's just that I have to keep chasing it, and I've really got better things to do.'

Just then, the man the other side of Nicholas started up a conversation with him, and we did not get a chance to speak further during the remainder of the meal. By the time coffee was served, copious amounts of wine had been consumed, and the tone of the conversation round our table went markedly

43

downhill, with one man in particular regaling us with a series of distinctly off-colour jokes and one-liners until he finally came out with an old crack: 'Why is it so hard for women to find men that are sensitive, caring and good looking? Because all those men already have boyfriends.'

There was an uncomfortable pause and I could feel several pairs of eyes swivelling in my direction, intrigued as to how I would react. By a stroke of luck, I happened to remember that the guy in question had recently been messily and expensively divorced for the second time, and I managed to reply in an even tone: 'Why are hurricanes normally named after women? When they come they're wild and wet, but when they go they take your house and car with them.'

There was a loud guffaw at this and my tormentor flushed a deep scarlet. By mutual telepathy the table broke up, and I followed Tom out to one of the boxes.

'Sorry about that, Ben,' said Tom as we leant over the rail to watch the horses assembling for the start, 'I don't think it was personal.'

'Oh, I know, I expect you're right,' I replied. 'It's just that I think I'm being got at from all quarters today.'

In response to his quizzical look, I quickly gave him a synopsis of the newspaper review, followed by the little incident with Keith Huxley.

Tom put a brotherly arm round my shoulder and said, 'Oh, well, don't worry about it all. Anyway, I thought you were great in the show. I felt like giving you a warm hand on your opening!'

Sometimes, I think Tom sails a little too near the wind for a straight man…

The afternoon passed by pleasantly. It was quite a jolly group in our box. There was a plentiful supply of drinks in one corner, and the sun shone. Tom and I, having a knowledge of horses equating to zero, formed a sort of syndicate, and by dint of watching the odds and a few gut-feelings, found ourselves modestly in profit by the end of the racing.

The only cloud on that particular horizon was the appearance of Keith Huxley from time to time to chat up his existing, and presumably potential, clients. I could tell that he was not overly thrilled that I was there. And to be fair, I would have probably felt the same in his position: nobody wants to invite the lion into their own den, so to speak.

I said as much to Tom, who thumped me in the back, and said that he had never regarded me as a lion, more of a pussycat, and proceeded to laugh loudly. I had to say that I failed to see the funny side of that remark and went off in a huff to refill my glass. I found myself standing next to a slightly built man of around thirty who was helping himself to a tonic water.

'Good idea,' I said, nodding in the direction of his glass. 'It's really not good to drink alcohol all afternoon, is it?'

He gave a nod. I thrust a hand out to him. 'I don't think we've met before, have we? My name's Ben. Ben Jonson.'

He gave a sort of start and tonic water slopped on the floor. He bent down to mop it up with a paper napkin that he had in one hand then straightened and held out his hand to clutch mine. It was clammy and cold, like a dead fish. He hadn't yet spoken, so I went on, 'And you are…?'

He gave another slight jump, then pulled himself together and mumbled, 'Oh, yes, sorry. I'm Douglas. Well, Doug, really.'

'And a surname? Oh, don't tell me! Doug Holes? Or possibly Doug Graves?' I chortled at my own wit.

He looked at me blankly.

'No, Doug Smith in point of fact.'

I felt suitably flattened. There was a pause, then a thought struck me, and I said, 'Doug? Do you work for Keith then?'

He hesitated for a split second, as though considering whether to answer this or not, but said, 'Yes, that's right. I'm one of his managers.'

Aha, I thought, *so this is the evasive Douglas that Nicholas Emmett was going on about.*

'It must be interesting work,' I said by way of keeping the conversational ball in play.

But Douglas returned it straight back with no spin by saying, 'If you will excuse me, I must go and see someone,' and hurried off, leaving me intrigued.

When I had mentioned my name, there was no doubt he had jumped and a look had crossed his face. *What was it? Surprise? Fear? Or*, I wondered, *guilt?*

I was still wondering as I absentmindedly poured myself another glass of chardonnay, abjuring my good intentions and found it was my turn to jump as a voice behind me said:

'"Drink to me, only with thine eyes
And I will pledge with mine…"'

It was Tom, who was by now looking slightly the worse for wear, quoting my illustrious namesake.

I fixed him with a steely glare and carried on:

'"Drink today, and drown all sorrow;
You shall perhaps not do it tomorrow!"'

Tom grinned and said, 'Not much fear of that! Come on, time we were off. I'll call Roddy and tell him to come and get us. Let's hope my car's all right!'

We made our way out of the box and sought out Keith to say our thank yous and make our farewells. To be fair to Keith, he was very gracious, though I had the feeling it was with gritted teeth as far as I was concerned. And he light-heartedly made a remark to Tom not to bring the competition with him next time.

The faithful Roddy soon pulled up at the entrance and we climbed in, though not before Tom had cast an eye around the bodywork to satisfy himself that there was no damage. As we drove along, I asked Tom what he knew about Keith.

'Oh, much the same as you, I expect,' he began airily. 'Quite charming, but I think he's able and hardworking in spite of that. Must be loaded too, I should imagine.'

'Do you have many dealings with him professionally?' I asked.

Tom considered this. 'Not a vast amount. He sends a few of his clients to us for this and that – you know, wills and general estate planning things – but nothing of any consequence.'

'And what about the other way round? Do you give him anything?'

Tom looked at me with a half-smile. 'Not getting jealous are we, old boy?'

I shook my head, although I could feel the colour rising in my cheeks. I hated to admit it, even to myself, but I didn't like the thought of Tom giving work to Keith.

Tom was continuing. 'We only give him odds and ends, and only stuff which you wouldn't want. Of course, what Keith really is after is my firm's account...' I opened my mouth to say something, but Tom swept on, 'but naturally, he won't get it, because we're perfectly happy with you and your lot, my dear chap. Satisfied?' He gave me a playful punch in the arm.

I said, with a rueful smile, 'Yes, OK. I was wondering why he invited you – plus a friend, to the races today.'

After a second I asked, 'On another tack, do you know anything about Keith's sidekick, Douglas Smith?'

Tom looked mildly surprised. 'Can't say I do. Why?'

'Oh, no particular reason,' I replied, 'Just that his name came up in conversation, and then I bumped into him. Seemed a bit odd, I thought.'

Roddy gave a slight cough at this juncture. 'Sorry to butt in,' he said, 'but I know Doug a bit. He lives round the corner from me.'

'And?' I enquired.

'Well, I suppose he is a bit odd. But I feel kind of sorry for him. He's stuck with his mother who's an invalid – has to have carers all the time.'

'What's wrong with her?' I asked.

'Not sure,' replied Roddy, 'I think someone said it was dementia or something. But she has to have 24-hour care.'

'That must cost a bit,' I said.

'Typical!' Tom intervened, 'First thing you think of is the bottom line!'

There was a momentary pause at this, whilst Roddy stifled a snigger, and Tom coloured. 'Oops, sorry, I didn't mean...' he stammered.

'Don't worry, no offence taken,' I replied with as much dignity as I could muster.

Fortunately, we had reached my office by this point, so I took my leave, declining an offer of further drinks at Et Alia. Deciding that I had no real need to go in to the building, I rattled the door to check it was locked and walked the three hundred yards back home.

When I let myself in, Marcus was already home and waved a wine glass at me. I shook my head and said, 'No thanks, what I really want is a nice cup of tea!'

He looked startled at this, and so I explained to him the events of the day.

'Well, it's all right for some,' he remarked. 'The rest of us have had to do some work today!'

'But at least you haven't been trashed in the press and then insulted left right and centre!' I retorted, going to tell him about the review in The Clarion and the unfortunate remarks at the races.

Marcus was duly sympathetic. 'Dear Ben, forget about it. Have your tea, and then I'll get us something to eat.'

After a night's sleep, I felt better and was quite touched when I got to the office to find a very effusive email from Tom, hoping that he hadn't offended me. I sent an equally effusive one back, assuring him that he hadn't, and thanking him for the previous day's entertainment.

A faint sound of singing made me look up from my desk.

'If ever, ever, ever
They get back to Spain,
They will never, never, never
Cross the sea again!
They will never, never, never, never, never, never, never,
never, never, never, never
Cross the sea again!'

It was Janet, obviously limbering up for the auditions for *The Gondoliers*, the next extravaganza for the operatic society. This set me thinking: did I want to try for a part and face the possible humiliation of not passing the audition, or worse, having a part and being vilified in the press. Or should I just rein in my ambitions and forget all about CAOS, for the time being at least? I was mulling this dilemma over in my head when the phone rang. It was Nicolas Emmett.

'Would you believe it?' he began, 'Another letter this morning from the school with a not-so-gentle reminder about the fees!'

'Have you spoken to Keith about this?' I asked.

Nicholas snorted. 'Not today, I haven't. But I have on previous occasions. And to that Douglas what's-his-name. In fact, last time I said that if they didn't sort themselves out, I'd take my business elsewhere.'

'Mmm,' I pondered for a moment, then said, 'You didn't say where you might go by any chance, did you?'

Nicholas replied promptly, 'I certainly did. I said I'd go straight to you.'

Well, that explains why Keith and Douglas didn't look overly thrilled to see me the previous day, I thought.

'Nicholas, do you think you could come down to my office soon? And bring all the records you can relating to this trust you mentioned.'

Nicholas said he would do that as soon as he could, and before he rang off I asked, 'And Nicholas, could I ask a favour of you, please?'

I tried to settle down to work after this conversation, but found my mind drifting. It wasn't helped by Janet, who seemed to be in a determinedly bombastic mood, and kept sweeping into my office, singing away:

'*If ever, ever, ever*
They get back to Spain,
They will never, never, never
Cross the sea again!'

After the third such intrusion, I remonstrated with her. 'Janet, please! You're disturbing my train of thought!'

Janet stopped singing, and gave me one of her steely stares.

'Looks to me as though the train, as you call it, has hit the buffers!' she riposted.

'Not at all!' I protested, but she swept on.

'Look,' she said, 'a bus station is where a bus stops. A train station is where a train stops. On your desk, you have a work station.'

I had to acknowledge the truth of this, and gave a rueful smile.

'Come on,' she said in a softer tone, 'What's the problem?'

'Well, two problems really,' I replied, and quickly outlined my conversations with Nicholas. 'But more immediately,' I went on, 'it's what to do about the auditions, for *The Gondoliers*. After that piece in The Clarion I'm not sure I want to carry on.'

'Oh, take no notice of that!' Janet said airily. 'It's only a little provincial rag. Anyway, the guy from the Echo said you were really quite passable.'

I was just about to reply that I didn't consider that comment to be exactly a paean of praise when the phone rang. Janet snatched up the receiver and listened, then pressing "mute" said, 'It's Keith Huxley. Do you want to take the call?'

I paused for a second. I scented trouble here. It could not be coincidence that so soon after my conversations with Nicholas, Keith should take it into his head to call. But I decided it was best to tackle him head-on, so I nodded at Janet and took the receiver off her.

'Good morning, Keith,' I said as breezily as I could. 'What an unexpected pleasure!'

'This is not a social call, Ben,' Keith said shortly. I had a feeling it wouldn't be.

'What can I do for you then, Keith?' I went on.

'Well, I expect you might know that I've just had a conversation with Nicholas Emmett in which he told me that he wants to transfer all his affairs to your outfit.'

'Oh yes?' I replied in an even tone.

'Yes, and I consider it highly unethical that you accept my hospitality, then poach clients from me. Highly unethical!'

I started to explain, but Keith had now got the bit between his teeth, and went on at some length before ending with a threat to report me and my firm to the institute.

'Well, you must do as you see fit, Keith,' I replied coolly, and put the phone down.

I hoped I sounded more confident than I felt: talk of reporting to the institute always filled me with absolute horror. But in truth, when I thought about it, what was there to say? A client of Keith's had approached me because he was not happy with Keith's firm. It was not that I had gone out of my way to poach Keith's client, though I had to admit, the timing, just after I'd accepted (albeit at second-hand) Keith's hospitality at the races, was a bit unfortunate.

The incident hung over me all day like a dark shadow and I was glad when it was time to leave the office. I gave Marcus a call and suggested we meet in Et Alia where I thought there was a fair chance of bumping into Tom and perhaps some of his cronies. And so it was that an hour later we were seated in a quiet corner of the wine bar and I had been telling the others of my hesitation about the forthcoming auditions.

Marcus asked, 'What part would you really like to play?'

'The Duke of Plaza-Toro, of course,' I replied promptly, 'though I think it's unlikely I'd get that. It's written for a baritone, or I suppose more accurately, a *comic* baritone. I'm a tenor.'

'Is that a *comic* tenor then?' asked Marcus, 'because you make me laugh!'

'Oh, ha, ha, very amusing!' I replied sarcastically.

Tom interrupted. 'What's the Duke's big song in that operetta then?'

I replied that it was *In Enterprise of Martial Kind* and sang a few lines:

'In enterprise of martial kind,
When there was any fighting,
He led his regiment from behind—
He found it less exciting…'

'Oh, yes, I remember,' said Tom, 'wait, let me think a minute…'

He and Marcus went into a huddle and started scribbling on a piece of paper, which after a short while, they pushed in my direction.

'Go on!' they cried, 'Do that at your audition. You're bound to get it then!'

I looked at the piece of paper, then started to sing:

'In enterprise of any kind
When there is fraud suspected
We send our skilful team along
And do our best to detect it,
We go through lots and lots of files
And evidence is collected,
The sober-suited
Un-saluted
Instituted
Jonson's
Forensical Accountants.
We always get results, clearly,
We really are the best, you see!
The sober-suited
Un-saluted
Instituted
Jonson's
Forensical Accountants!'

I finished to wild applause.

I studied the documents that Nicholas had brought in. They were incomplete, but I could see from the few bank statements that he had given me that around April each year, there were unidentified sums of money going in then out of the main account. I managed also in one year to find a more complete set. When I looked at the beginning of each school term, there seemed to be very little in the account, but then, usually some weeks later, a deposit would be made, which more or less equalled the school fees which were paid out.

The suspicion that had been forming in my mind ever since the encounter with Nicholas at the races was now more or less confirmed. The bank account of the trust had been subject to a type of "teeming and lading" as we term it in accountancy circles. Teeming and lading is a bookkeeping fraud also known as short banking or delayed accounting. It involves the allocation of one client's payment or account balance to another in order to make the books balance and often in order to hide a shortfall or theft. The big question, of course: who was the perpetrator?

'You're looking very thoughtful.' Janet's sudden interjection made me jump. Once again, I cursed the open door policy which had allowed her to creep up on me undetected. However, she is generally quite shrewd, so I decided to share my thoughts with her.

When I'd finished, she said, 'So you think that this Doug Smith is responsible?'

I leaned back and arched my fingers together in my best professorial manner.

'Well,' I said, 'I suppose he must be the prime suspect.' I leaned forward again and started ticking points off on my hands.

'Firstly, he's got the opportunity. According to Nicholas, he, or at least someone in the firm, has access to the bank accounts and can make payments electronically. Secondly, he probably is the one who prepares accounts and so on, and is therefore in a position to manipulate the figures if need be. Thirdly, he's got a motive.'

'What's the motive?' queried Janet.

I gave a lofty laugh and said, 'Everyone could use more money, couldn't they?'

Janet shrugged. 'I suppose so.'

'But,' I went on, 'he, that is, Doug Smith, has a particular need for money' I explained about his mother needed constant carers. 'And,' I finished, 'that sort of thing doesn't come cheap. I don't suppose, even as a manger, that he earns that much.'

'So what are you going to do about it?' Janet fixed with me with one of her gimlet looks.

I considered. Finally I said, 'Well, I need more proof. I need to show for one thing that there has in fact been an actual loss to the trust's funds. We're still waiting for all the stuff from Huxleys.'

'Nicholas has actually told them that he wants you to act?'

'Yes, he apparently mentioned it to them even before he'd seen me that day at the races. Now, he has formally told them and asked them to provide me with everything. Though we're still waiting for all that – what I've got is only what Nicholas happened to have.'

'Have you said anything about all this to Nicholas?' The gimlet bored into me once again.

'Not yet,' I replied. Again, I was met with that look and went on defensively, 'Well, I may be wrong. It wouldn't do to cause a big fuss if, in fact, nothing was wrong, would it?'

Janet merely sniffed. The Methodist upbringing was once more to the fore. She left the room, though as she went, I distinctly heard her murmur, 'All that is necessary for evil to succeed is that good men do nothing.'

Thank you, Edmund Burke, I thought grimly, *though I suppose at least Janet must think I'm a good man.*

I've quite often found that when I am in a quandary about what to do in a particular situation, not doing anything is often the best course. "Masterly inactivity" as Marcus puts it, adding rather pointedly that I seem to have a particular talent in that direction. I prefer to regard it in more whimsical terms, and liken myself to the peers in *Iolanthe*, who,

> *'throughout the war*
> *Did nothing in particular*
> *And did it very well.'*

And so it turned out.

The following day, an email popped up on my screen, declaring itself to come from none other than the lugubrious Doug Smith. It stated that he had collected the records of the trust together and would drop them off at my office that afternoon on his way home, if that was convenient. I swiftly replied that it was.

Around five-thirty, Janet, who was on the point of leaving put her head round the door and said, 'Douglas Smith from Huxleys is here with a box, and he said could he have a quick word with you?'

Surprised, I indicated agreement, and a moment or two later, Janet showed him in.

'Have a pew!' I indicated a chair in my most uxorious manner.

Douglas looked uncertain, but lowered himself gingerly into a chair opposite my desk.

There was a pause, and in order to cover the silence, I thanked him for bringing the records over. He looked as though he was struggling to know what to say, then eventually said slowly, 'You will go through the box of stuff carefully to make sure you have everything you need, won't you?'

I assured him that my staff would see to that.

He looked alarmed. 'No, no,' he cried, 'I really think you should do it yourself. You can't be too careful, can you?'

Somewhat mystified, I agreed that indeed, you cannot be too careful. After another pause, I asked, 'I suppose you're on your way home?'

Douglas nodded.

'And someone was telling me that your mother is…er…unwell?'

Again Douglas nodded, but added, 'Yes, she needs constant care now.'

'Oh, I'm sorry to hear that,' I continued, in a tone of deep sympathy, then as an opportunity to probe struck me, added, 'I suppose that must be terribly expensive?'

He looked at me slightly strangely, then said, 'I certainly couldn't afford it on my salary. Fortunately for us, my mother is beneficiary of a trust which has plenty of money.'

I felt somewhat chastened. It seemed as though Douglas had guessed what I had been thinking and done his best to rebut it. As he left, he again urged me to look through the box myself.

I collected the box from where Janet had placed it in our records room, and returned to my desk. 'Bang goes the glass of wine with Tom at the wine bar,' I thought as I settled down to work. Obviously, Douglas wanted me to find something in particular.

I sifted through piles of accounts, bank statements, computer print-outs and more, until my eye fell on a sheet of paper tucked between two old ledgers. A brief glance and I gave an involuntary intake of breath. This was it – the smoking gun!

Again, as I sat back in my chair wondering what to do next, events overtook me. My mobile rang, and as I picked it up, I saw it was a call from my old friend Tom Bremner.

As I started to answer, his voice boomed out, 'Where the hell are you, Ben? You're wasting good drinking time!'

Before I could finish explaining, he interrupted, 'Never mind that, come over now.'

He rang off before I could ask any questions, and so I pulled my jacket on, locked up the office and made my way along the high street to Et Alia. Tom was there in our usual corner and talking to a man with his back towards me. The man looked vaguely familiar and at the sound of my greeting, he swung around. It was none other than Keith Huxley.

To say that he looked less than thrilled to see me would be a gross understatement. I too was taken aback and I could cheerfully have hit Tom for not saying who his drinking companion was, but I managed a reasonably civil greeting. Tom volunteered to go to the bar to get the drinks, and I took advantage of his absence to say casually, 'Thanks for getting Nicholas' things over to me. They arrived this afternoon.'

Keith looked at me steadily for a moment.

'Then you won't have had a chance to look through them?' he asked.

'Well actually, *au contraire,*' I replied, 'I've had a good look.'

I fixed him with a gimlet stare that would have made Janet envious.

'Really?' He tried to sound nonchalant.

'And so I know,' I went on.

'Know?'

'Yes,' I replied, 'I know. Not perhaps how much, or if there are any others, but I know enough.'

His eyes narrowed. 'I don't know what you're talking about,' he began, but I cut him off.

'Oh, I think you do. And the question is, are you going to the police voluntarily, or do I have to tell them to come and arrest you?'

He hesitated for only a second, 'Make my excuses to Tom, will you?' he said lightly as he slid out of his chair and made for the exit.

Just at that moment, Tom returned with the drinks.

'Where the hell's Keith gone? I've got a large shiraz for him here!'

'In the words of *Ruddigore*, I think "he has recovered his forgotten moral senses",' I replied, 'though it is possible he's going to care more than tuppence ha'penny for the consequences.'

I didn't have to wait long for further news.

The next morning, Nicholas came on the line in a highly excitable state.

'I've just had the police on,' he started, 'you'll never guess what!'

'Try me!' I responded dryly.

'Keith Huxley's been arrested. He apparently walked into a police station last night and confessed to several counts of embezzlement, including from our trust. Not sure how much he's taken.'

'Around £52,000 according to my rough calculations,' I replied.

There was a pause.

'You already knew?' Nicholas asked.

'Well, not knew, but I had an idea.' I explained what had happened.

'Mmm,' he mused, 'well, thank you for putting the squeeze on him. I'm very grateful.'

'Not at all,' I replied. 'Oh, and that favour I asked of you? Well, more of your wife, really...'

'I'm on to it right now!' Nicholas replied cheerfully.

Not surprisingly, Tom was all agog when I walked into Et Alia that evening. I apologised for being a little later than normal, explaining that I had had an urgent appointment. In fact, there was quite a crowd, as Marcus had arrived as well, and unusually. Janet had for once forsaken her Methodist principles and was nursing what looked like a Pinot Grigio – a large one to boot.

Tom was first off the blocks. 'Come on, come on. Tell us all,' he began impatiently, 'when did you first suspect?'

I tried to look suitably modest, but I have a feeling I was not wholly successful. 'Well, I suppose at the races. As soon as Nicholas started talking about the school fees, my suspicions were aroused. It's such a classic example of what happens when someone starts stealing money.'

'But did you think it was Keith?'

Janet interrupted. 'No, he didn't. He thought it was Keith Huxley's sidekick, Douglas what's-his-name.'

I had to acknowledge the truth of this. 'Well, he seemed the most likely,' I tried to justify myself. 'He had the access to everything and I thought he had a particular motive.' I explained about Douglas' mother.

'But,' I went on, 'he said that there was money from a trust for that. I suppose he could have been lying, but he seemed genuine enough.'

'So what led you to think it was Keith?'

'Well, two things. Of course, if it wasn't Douglas, then really the next most obvious person would have to be Keith, for the same reasons – he would have access to the funds etc. But I wouldn't have thought he had need of the money. But, when Douglas came, he made such a point of ensuring that I went through the box of stuff myself that I realised he must have put something in there for me to find.'

'And did you?' The three of them spoke as one.

'Yes, eventually. It was just a single sheet, but it was a letter addressed to Keith from a mortgage company, threatening foreclosure if he didn't pay them the arrears.'

'So?'

'And so that meant that Keith must have been very short of money to have let things get to that state. Which, of course, means that he had the motive for taking money.'

'How did the letter come to be there?' Tom asked curiously.

'I guess that Douglas came across it somehow, probably by accident,' I replied.

'But why didn't he just confront Keith himself?' Marcus spoke this time, 'I would have thought that would be the obvious thing to do.'

I sighed. 'I don't know. Perhaps he was scared of being implicated, perhaps he was scared of Keith. Or perhaps it was out of some sort of loyalty. He didn't want to point the finger at Keith directly, but he knew something had to be done.'

'Did he know? Or was he involved himself?' Janet leaned forward in her chair.

I shrugged. 'I don't believe so. I think he didn't know for sure, but suspected something. I imagine that he queried some of the movements in the accounts, and Keith fobbed him off with some story. Probably it was OK for a while, but then Douglas started to wonder.'

'The other thing is,' said Tom with a furrowed brow, 'what happened to the money Keith took? It's not very bright, is it, to steal money and still end up with mortgage arrears.'

'I think a lot of it went on wine, women and song to coin a phrase' I replied, noting Janet's lips tighten in an expression of disapproval, 'although he probably didn't do much in the way of singing! He was in with a set who liked the high life. And he wanted to keep up with them, wining, dining, cars, holidays, and so on. And the practice can't have been as profitable as he used to make out.'

'But why did this all come out now?' Tom asked

I tried again to look modest. 'I think it was a conversation Nicholas had with Keith last week, just before the races. Nicholas apparently told Keith that he was not happy and was going to move his stuff to me. And I suppose he thought I might just find something wrong. So that, of course, is why he was less than pleased to see me at the races.'

Tom nodded. 'That's certainly true.'

'And what about that review of *Pirates*,' said Janet, 'didn't you say that it was done by Keith's son?'

I gave a wry grin. 'Well, supposedly. But according to Clive, the son only stayed about twenty minutes. And then Clive's chum at The Clarion told him that the piece was actually filed by Keith himself. He probably saw it as divine intervention or something – a way to get at me. Or perhaps it was just accurate reporting…?'

I paused, waiting for the cries of "no, no" "shameful" or some such. They did come, but perhaps slightly later than I would have liked…

It was a few days later, and our final performance of *The Pirates of Penzance*. In one of those magical moments of theatre, everything went perfectly – no missed cues, costume malfunctions or misspeaking, and we closed to thunderous applause, and even a standing ovation.

This latter, I had some suspicions, may have been prompted by loyal followers such as Marcus and Tom, who had been inveigled into coming to watch again, largely on the promise of a "session" at Et Alia' after the show, I have to confess. Be that as it may, it was all quite gratifying, and in the dressing room afterwards, Janet and Clive were very complimentary.

'You couldn't have been better, dear boy,' Clive breathed, his hands going up together in mock applause. I thought that this could have been taken two ways, but Clive went on, 'I've never seen such an improvement over the course of the run.'

I tried to look modest. 'Thank you Clive. Perhaps it's due to my secret weapon.'

'Secret weapon?' Clive looked perplexed.

'Yes,' I replied, 'my secret weapon, aka Mrs Nicholas Emmett.'

Clive looked blank for a moment. 'Ah,' he said finally, 'I see. You mean, Mrs Nicholas Emmett, the singing and drama teacher?'

'Exactly!' I replied.

Janet looked knowing. 'So that explains all those mysterious appointments at five o'clock each afternoon. You were having lessons.'

I nodded.

'Well, that seems to have paid off handsomely,' Clive beamed at me.

I smiled back at him.

'Yes, well, as they say in *The Gondoliers*,
*"Quiet calm deliberation
disentangles every knot."'*

3. Ben Jonson and a Woman Scorned

It was a warm and sunny Friday afternoon in late summer. The church clock was just chiming out five o'clock and I was contemplating calling it a day and retreating for a glass or two of Vino Collapso at our local wine bar, Et Alia, when Janet, my ferocious office manager, appeared in front of my desk with an armful of papers.

'Oh no, Janet, what's this?' I groaned, 'I've got an urgent appointment with a bottle of chardonnay right now.'

Janet's already thin lips tightened even further as her non-conformist upbringing asserted itself once again. 'Month end!' she exclaimed, dumping the pile on my desk. 'We need to go through the invoicing and write-offs so that I can get on with it.'

'Can't we do it on Monday?' I pleaded.

Janet withered me with a look. 'No, we can't,' she snapped back and glared at me over the top of her glasses.

I was about to protest again, but she silenced me with another glare. 'Oh well,' I said, 'we'd better get on with it, I suppose.'

An hour later, we had finished, and Janet stood up and gathered the mass of paper.

'Right, well, you can go off to the wine bar now,' she said in the tone of a primary school teacher dismissing her class. Sometimes I wonder who is the boss around here...

I got up from my desk as she left, but before I had a chance to escape, she swung round at the door and said, 'Oh, there was one other thing.'

My heart sank.

'Oh yes?' I replied 'What was that?'

'Do you remember that conversation we had the other week?'

'Which particular one would that be?' I said, trying to keep the impatience out of my voice.

Janet carried on, 'The one where I said that I thought we needed to update our image.'

It was my turn for a tightening of the lips. I recalled the conversation only too well. Janet had blithely said one day that she thought my firm's stationery and logo were too staid and boring and needed to be changed. When I replied in a rather testy fashion that I had designed them myself, she had said, 'Well, obviously,' leaving me seething with rage.

She had also said that we needed a slogan or by-line on all the signage "to try to bring us up to date". I had, of course, totally ignored all that. But Janet is like a terrier with a rat once she has an idea, and will keep worrying at it for ever.

'Oh yes, I do vaguely remember,' I said in an airy tone.

Janet grimaced.

'Yes, well, I knew *you* wouldn't do anything about it,' she retorted, 'so I've had a few designs drawn up.' She thrust a package into my hands. 'And whilst I was about it,' she went on, 'I had a little competition in the office here for the staff to come up with a catchy slogan.'

'Oh, joy unbounded!' I said, in an ironic reference to Gilbert & Sullivan.

Janet affected not to notice the irony and handed me another file. 'Here you are,' she said, 'you can look through them over the weekend and let me know what you think on Monday morning.'

The teacher, having set the class its homework, exited with a sniff.

I had managed, even under the eagle eye of Janet, to send an email to Marcus, suggesting we meet at Et Alia and was relieved to find him sitting at one of the tables on the small terrace, enjoying the early evening sun. I was even more relieved to see that he had pre-empted me and had ordered a large glass of white wine.

'My goodness, I'm ready for this,' I exclaimed as I sat down and we clinked glasses in salutation.

'Bad day?' Marcus asked, tilting his head to one side.

'Oh, not really, I suppose,' I replied, 'just that Janet was getting on my wick a bit.' I swiftly explained the events of the last hour.

'Let's have a look at these things then,' Marcus said, taking the packages from me.

Marcus works in marketing, so has a good handle on these things. He swiftly sifted through the letterhead and logo mock-ups which Janet had produced, selecting two which he placed on the table. 'These are really rather good,' he said, 'what do you think, Ben?'

I snorted. 'Waste of time, effort and money, if you ask me. Nothing wrong with what we've got.'

Marcus sighed. 'Don't be so prickly, Ben. I know you designed the existing ones, but that must have been quite a few years ago. Time for a change, perhaps?'

'Possibly,' I answered gruffly.

I glanced at the designs. I had to grudgingly admit that they were very stylish.

'Let's look at these slogans,' Marcus went on in an encouraging tone. He opened the file and started reading. After a minute or two, he threw the file down on the table.

'Oh, my God,' he cried, closing his eyes in mock horror.

'That bad?' I queried.

'Worse than you could imagine,' Marcus confirmed, opening his eyes and rifling through the file

'Try me!'

'OK, you asked for it.' Marcus selected a sheet. 'How about this one:

"Come to us,

We're the force,

To keep your figures

Right on course.'"

I groaned.

'Or how about this,' Marcus pressed on ruthlessly, 'here's a cracker:

"Don't leave it all and trust to fate,
Leave it to us to calculate."'

'Who the hell wrote that one?' I snatched the paper out of his hand. 'Good grief, it's signed "Alice in Ledgerland". I suppose that would be Alison in Business Services.'

Marcus laughed. 'Well, the first one was done by a whole department, apparently. "Payrolls 'R' Us" so it says.'

'Mmmm,' I said, lips tightening in a fair imitation of Janet's, 'I somehow get the feeling that they weren't taking this exercise entirely seriously.'

'Well, let's hope not!' Marcus laughed once more, 'Come on, I'll go and get another round in.'

Monday morning came round in a blink of an eye, and I had barely time to sit down before Janet appeared before me, like a genie out of a bottle.

'Ah, morning, Jeannie, I mean Janet,' I corrected myself hastily, 'and what can I do for you this fine day?'

Janet ignored my pleasantries and went straight for the jugular, so to speak, like the terrier she is.

'I expect you haven't even looked at those designs and things I gave you the other day, have you?' she barked.

I leaned back in my chair and put the fingers of both hands together. 'Well, in point of fact,' I said, in my most supercilious tone, 'I have. And what is more,' I went on, before Janet could leap in, 'I have chosen the design.'

I selected a piece of paper from the folder on my desk, and pushed it towards her. *That'll take the wind out of your sails*, I thought to myself.

'Oh, right, yes, well, very good,' she started, looking suitably deflated.

I pressed on before she could say more. 'The only point I haven't decided on is the choice of the slogan. To be honest, I thought they were all a load of rubbish.'

Janet looked mildly surprised. 'What? Even mine?

"Streets ahead of all the rest,
For your books,
we're the best."'

'Yes,' I said firmly, 'even that.'

The lips tightened once more. 'And have you got one?' Janet fixed me with one of her looks.

I had to confess that I hadn't come up with anything particularly catchy. 'But I'm working on it,' I protested , 'and I've asked Marcus to apply the grey matter to it as well. So I'm sure we'll produce something.'

Janet eyed me dubiously, but just then, the phone rang, and she snatched up the receiver before I could get to it.

'Tom Bremner for you,' she said after a pause and passed me the phone with a hint of a shudder. I don't think she entirely approves of Tom, my drinking companion at Et Alia and a profitable source of business.

'Morning, Ben,' Tom's *basso profundo* boomed in my ear. 'Busy?'

'Always busy, Tom,' I said, then added in my most obsequious manner, 'but never too busy to talk to you!'

'Easy with the smarm, Jonson,' Tom barked back.

'Fair enough,' I laughed, 'so what can I do for you?'

'Well, it's more what I can do for you,' he replied. 'Got an interesting little case here, which might be right up your street. Divorce case, in fact.'

'Divorce?' I expressed surprise, 'Not your usual field of expertise, Tom.'

'No, true, it isn't. Been passed to me by one of my partners. It's to do with the financial side, as you might have guessed.'

"Anything in particular?" I asked.

'Well,' Tom sounded hesitant, 'there is a private company involved, so you might need to look at the valuations the other side have come up with.'

'OK, the normal sort of thing,' I paused for a second, 'but I get the distinct feeling that there is something more that you're not saying.'

'You're right of course,' Tom sighed, 'you see, the thing is, our client – by the way, we're acting for the wife, a Mrs Rosamund Thurstan, née Cotterill – she claims that her husband is not declaring all his assets to the court.'

'Ah, I see,' I gave a rueful laugh. 'It sounds like an attack of that troublesome condition, SADS.'

'SADS?' Tom sounded at sea.

'Yes, SADS. Or to put in more clearly, "Sudden Asset Deficiency Syndrome". And of course, it's usually accompanied by its sister condition, SIDS, or "Sudden Income Deficiency Syndrome".'

'Right, I see, yes. SIDS and SADS. Thank you *so* much, Ben.' Tom was always a bit heavy-handed with the irony.

'Anyway,' he went on briskly, 'I'll send the files across and let you get stuck in. Should be interesting for you, as the husband is claiming he's in Queer Street.' There was a pause. Then he said hurriedly, 'Whoops, sorry, Ben, I didn't mean...'

'It's OK, Tom, no offence taken,' I said firmly, though I thought as I put the phone down that these Freudian slips by Tom were getting more frequent...

I had a day with more or less back to back meetings, so it was getting on for five o'clock before I returned to my office. I found on my desk a parcel which I guessed would contain the papers in Thurstan v. Thurstan. I had scarcely opened the package and established that my surmise had been correct, when Janet appeared before me.

'How does, "We work hard for you, We don't relax, Till we've minimised, All your tax", grab you?' she fired off.

Momentarily confused, I said, 'It doesn't grab me, as you put it, at all. What are you on about?'

Janet rolled her eyes heavenwards, then in a tone of exaggerated patience said, 'As a slogan. You know, for our new image.'

Light dawned. 'Oh, that thing. Well, frankly, Janet, I think it may be better to leave it to the experts, like Marcus, and not waste our time on it.'

The lips tightened once again. She went on: 'Or there's always, "We're looking at your bottom line."'

I leaned back in my chair. 'That,' I said coldly, 'is perilously close to impertinence!'

Janet looked as though she was about to argue, but then thought better of it. In a more conciliatory tone, she said, 'Don't forget, it's the start of auditions tonight for *The Gondoliers*. What part are you hoping for?'

I didn't reply for a moment or two. The memories of my last appearance in one of CAOS' productions were still a little raw. Although the final performance had been something of a triumph, I could not completely forget the terrible reviews the local paper had given me earlier on. This was despite the fact that the reviewer had turned out to be an old business rival of mine with a distinct axe to grind. I was far from eager to put my head into that particular lion's mouth again, so to speak.

'I'm not sure I want to try for a part on this occasion,' I eventually said.

If I was hoping for an expression of incredulity from Janet and an exhortation to delight the general public once more with my singular abilities, then I was sadly mistaken.

'Oh, fair enough,' she replied airily, 'there's a lot of talent around at the moment, so I doubt you'd get one of the leads anyway.'

I bridled at this. 'On the other hand,' I said in a pompous manner, 'I would hate to disappoint my public and let Clive, our director, down.'

Janet, probably with some justification, looked a little dubious at this, but confined herself to saying in an even tone, 'I dare say Clive would be able to get over the shock.'

I had to secretly confess to myself that Janet was probably correct in this last observation. Relations between Clive and I, often strained to say the least, had taken a turn for the worse at the closing night party of *The Pirates of Penzance*.

Tom and Marcus, who between them have a remarkable facility for writing alternative lyrics to well-known G&S songs, had produced a parody of the song *A Policeman's Lot* and I regret to say, fuelled by too much chardonnay, I had willingly performed it in our local wine bar, Et Alia.

The closing stanza went:

'Our first night and old Clive is feeling nervous (feeling nervous)
And you'll find him propped up against the bar ('gainst the bar)
It's on the basis if he drinks enough beforehand ('nough beforehand)
Then he might not notice just how bad we are (bad we are)

But in the end it all turned out to be quite marv'lous (quite marv'lous)
The ensemble didn't get a single thing wrong (thing wrong)
And Clive pranced around in reflected glory ('flected glory)
Saying, "I knew that they'd be brilliant all along!"'

Regrettably, Clive had failed to see the funny side, and whilst the company and regulars of the wine bar had fallen about laughing, he had marched off in something of a huff. I had felt obliged to do some grovelling to him the next day to try to smooth matters over.

Janet's stentorian tones interrupted my reverie. 'Right then, I'll be off. And perhaps I'll see you in the church hall?'

I nodded and Janet left with the hint of a sniff. I picked up the files once again and starting browsing through the papers. According to the notes, Rosamund Thurstan (née Cotterill) had been married to the exotically named Garnet Thurstan for twenty-five years, and the couple had been blessed with two children, a boy and a girl.

Garnet had been a chemical engineer but having been made redundant in the early years of the marriage, had started his own company which dealt in agrichemicals. The company had grown and prospered and Rosamund, who was a teacher by profession, had been able to retire from that field and become a lady of relative leisure. Although nominally the company secretary and a shareholder in the company, Thurstans Limited, she had taken virtually no part in the running of it, but was content to let the money roll in.

But then Garnet had employed as his PA a young lady by the name of Kelsey Nelson who, it turned out, had attributes other than a nice telephone manner and a passing knowledge of spreadsheets.

Indeed, it was quite a different type of sheet she seemed to have her eye on, I thought wryly.

As happens all too often, the older Garnet was captivated by the attentions of the young siren and soon announced to the distraught Rosamund that the marriage was over and he was moving in with *la belle* Kelsey. Adding to Rosamund's woes was Garnet's disclosure that Thurstans was no longer doing well and so her dividends and salary were to be cut.

I started making some notes, but soon saw that there was actually more to this than I had anticipated. Glancing at the clock, I decided that I would leave it there and continue in the morning. I just had time to lock up and make my way along the high street to the church hall in time for the auditions...

In fact, I was later than I thought, and the auditions were in full swing by the time I arrived. I pushed open the door of the hall just as there was a burst of rapturous applause. For one brief moment, I thought it was for me, and was trying to adopt a look of suitably becoming modesty when I realised that all eyes were facing the opposite direction. Just stepping down from the dais at the far end of the room was a good-looking, dark-haired man of around thirty, who, like me, seemed to be trying to adopt a look of self-deprecation. Again, like me I suspect, he was failing.

'Oh, bravo, Randall,' our director, Clive Pettit's voice could be heard as the clapping subsided, and his hands went up together in his characteristic manner.

'Bravo, Randall, that was marvellous,' Clive continued as I drew nearer. 'I think we can find you a place as one of the principle tenors. Though, to be honest,' he went on, lowering his voice in a confidential manner, 'the competition isn't really very strong, you know. In fact, the last production was a...oh, hello, Ben,' Clive suddenly paused as I appeared in his field of vision, 'I didn't see you there.'

'Obviously not,' I replied somewhat coolly.

Clive affected not to notice and said, 'Let me introduce you. Ben, this is a new recruit to CAOS, Randall Barrett. Randall, this is Ben Jonson, one of our older hands, as it were.'

I wasn't entirely sure I liked this description, but I took Randall's proffered hand and murmured "Pleased to meet you" in response. The younger man shook hands in that rather peculiar way some Americans have, of grasping your one hand then covering the two joined ones with their remaining hand. I suppose it is intended to convey additional sincerity to the enquiry, "How do you do?" but I find I instinctively react to it in exactly the opposite way, and regard the shakee (so to speak) with suspicion.

Randall still had my hand in his and was speaking. 'I am very pleased to meet you, sir,' he said, 'I've heard so much about you.'

'Well, you shouldn't necessarily believe everything you hear,' I replied, lightly enough, though through slightly gritted teeth. Being called "sir" in those circumstances also raised my hackles...

Clive interrupted us. 'Randall comes to us with lots of experience,' he enthused.

'Really?' I said, with a metaphorical, if not actual, raising of an eyebrow.

Randall again tried to look modest. 'Well, yes, I suppose so. I was Professor Higgins in *Pygmalion* at the Bath festival a couple of years ago – seemed to go down quite well. And I did *The Dream* in an outdoor production last summer.'

'What part?' I asked.

Randall looked me straight in the eye and replied, 'Bottom.'

It was one of those moments when time seems to stand still, and I had the impression of a long pause whilst various replies to this admission ran through my mind.

"Oh really," I could say, "and did you receive a big hand on your Bottom?" for instance, or even, "And was your Bottom widely admired?"

I considered these and weighed them up for what seemed like an age, before casting them aside as too camp, too rude or simply not funny, and settled on something more prosaic.

'Oh yes? And what about operetta? Any G&S?'

'Well, some. I've done most of the big ones, and most recently I was Marco in *The Gondoliers*.'

This was a bit of a nasty one, as Marco was the part I was after. If I am honest, I am probably getting a bit old at nearly fifty to be playing such roles, though I flatter myself that I still have a reasonable figure and a fairly unlined face. This together with a bit of make-up and the right lighting creates to my mind a not entirely unconvincing look.

As Marcus says, quoting *Trial by Jury*, "You may very well pass for forty-three in the dusk with the light behind you."

Clive interrupted us once more. 'Come on, boys, we must be getting on. Right, as you're here now, Ben, why don't you give us a turn?'

I went up to the dais, and after a nod to Betty, our pianist, launched into my song. When I had finished, there was some muted applause, though nothing like the reception that had been awarded to Randall.

'Thank you, Ben,' Clive said, giving a single clap in the air, 'we'll let you know.'

'Don't ring us, we'll ring you!' I thought to myself as I stomped down the room. A light tap on my shoulder made me swing round. It was Randall.

'I thought that was really good, sir,' he said with apparent sincerity.

I was momentarily surprised. 'Did you?' I replied.

'Yes, I did,' said Randall, 'I mean considering your…' I think he was going to say "considering your age" but he obviously thought better of it and carried on, 'I mean considering we don't have the orchestra or chorus here.'

'Oh well, thank you,' I replied, 'Anyway, must be going. Urgent appointment at the wine bar!'

I was just about to exit the room when I came across Janet.

'Have you met the new man, Randall?' she asked, looking somewhat starry-eyed. I nodded and she carried on, 'Isn't he marvellous? Such a terrific voice. And he can act too, not like…' I had a feeling she was about to say "not like you" but she went on, 'not like he's just a singer. And so good-looking. Lovely physique too…' she turned to look at Randall who was busily talking to Clive again, 'he'll be a real asset to the company.'

'Won't he just?' I replied in a clipped tone, 'I'm off to Et Alia. Can I buy you a drink?'

The lips tightened into a line. 'Certainly not!' she snapped, 'I've got to think of my vocal chords. And anyway, it's a weekday!'

The non-conformist upbringing had spoken.

I made my way further along the high street and entered the hallowed portals of Et Alia once again. As I had expected, I found Marcus and Tom sitting in our usual corner with a bottle in front of them and, I was relieved to see, three glasses.

'Make mine a large one!' I said wearily, sitting down with a sigh.

'Trouble?' Marcus looked at me sympathetically, whilst the ever-practical Tom poured out a large glass of chardonnay.

'I'll say!' I responded and told them all about the evening's events and my disquietude over the egregious Randall Barrett.

'Oh, don't worry about it!' Tom was typically dismissive, 'I'm sure there's plenty of parts for all of you.'

'You don't understand!' I exclaimed petulantly, 'I wanted the part of Marco and now I'm not likely to get it. You should have seen the way that Clive was fawning over that Randall. He thought he was the best thing since sliced bread.'

Marcus gave me that look of a patient adult toward a tiresome child, which only irritated me further.

'I'm going for a refill!' I said in a fit of pique and went off toward the bar. It was very crowded and it took me a little while to get served. When I returned to the table, I found Tom and Marcus with heads together, scribbling on a piece of paper, and giggling like naughty school kids.

'OK, OK, hand it over.' I stood over them and held my hand out. Still giggling, Tom passed me a sheet of paper, headed "To the tune of '*A Policeman's Lot*'".

I read the sheet:

'When Ben Jonson is attending an audition (an audition)
He strolls around with an air of nonchalance (nonchalance)
He thinks that there is little competition (competition)
And he can pick whichever part he wants (part he wants)

Our laughter we with difficulty smother ('culty smother)
As he struts around and thinks the lead he's won (he's won)
But then he finds the role's been given to another (to another)
To a lad who's young enough to be his son.

Oh, when a G&S production's to be done, to be done
Ben Jonson's lot is not a happy one (happy one)!'

As I read, I became aware of the two faces watching me, and their expressions turning from ones of mirth to anxiety. I tried to smile and laugh whilst simultaneously smarting inside. Was this how everyone saw me? A vain, self-obsessed man whom everyone can't wait to see come a cropper? I had been hurt enough by the excoriating review in the local paper, but that was by an (apparent) stranger. This was worse, to be chided, mocked even, by those closest to me.

Marcus must have sensed my feelings, and he came and sat beside me and put an arm around my shoulders.

'Come on, Ben. Don't take it all so seriously. You're supposed to be doing this am-dram thing for a bit of fun, not to make it your career, for God's sake.'

I looked back at him, his face only inches from mine. I could feel his warm, wine laden-breath on my skin. 'You're right,' I said finally, 'Of course you're right. I shouldn't be so sensitive.'

'And anyway,' Tom intervened in his usual bluff manner, 'you can give it out, can't you? So you have to learn to take it. What about the song we wrote about Clive? You were quick enough to say he was being a prima-donna.'

I grinned ruefully. 'I was going to say that was completely different, but yes, I suppose you're right.' Marcus gave me a squeeze and a light kiss on the head and Tom leaned forward as if to do the same, but thought better of it and confined himself to giving me a playful punch on the shoulder.

'That's more like it,' he said, then clearing his throat went on, 'Now, who's for another glass of vino?' and proceeded to replenish our glasses.

I had more or less recovered my self-composure by the following morning and I arrived early at my office in order to work on the Thurstan case. I had been there about an hour when Janet appeared before me, humming one of the songs from *The Gondoliers*. She didn't say anything, but stood in front of my desk, singing to herself and tapping her foot in time to the (imaginary) music. I deliberately didn't acknowledge her presence, wanting to see how long it would take her to speak, but after a minute or two, I decided I couldn't wait any longer.

'Ah Janet, Good Morning,' I said, looking up as though I had only just realised she was there.

'The Specialists in Double Entry,' she replied.

I blinked at this enigmatic opening.

'I beg your pardon?'

'"The Specialists in Double Entry",' she said rather snappily, 'The slogan. For the signage.'

I sighed. 'Not that again, Janet. I told you, let's leave it to the experts, should we? Anyway, I think "The Specialists in Double Entry" is rather open to being misconstrued, isn't it? A little too near the bone, so to speak?'

Janet sniffed. 'Well, I must say that interpretation never crossed my mind. "Evil is in the eye, or the ear, in this case, of the beholder",' I would say.'

I felt suitably reprimanded.

'Changing the subject,' she went on, 'I thought the auditions went terribly well, didn't you? That Randall was so good, wasn't he? Wonderful voice, wonderful presence, so good-looking, such charming manners...'

I interrupted this eulogy on the virtues of the unimpeachable Randall. 'What part did you get then?'

'Duchess of Plaza-Toro,' Janet responded promptly, 'which is what I was going for. How about you?'

'Still waiting to hear from Clive,' I replied smoothly, and Janet gave me a knowing look. I went on, 'I don't suppose you know if Randall was given anything, do you?'

Janet's face took on an expression which verged upon the sympathetic. 'I think someone said Marco,' she replied, 'though I could have got it wrong,' she added hastily, obviously having noted my frown of disappointment. 'No doubt Clive will send an email round later with the full list.'

'No doubt he will,' I replied gloomily.

I returned to my labours. I emailed one of my team to do some research on Thurstans at the Companies House site, and let me know the results. I buzzed Janet and asked her to make an appointment with Rosamund Thurstan to come in to the office. I always find there is nothing quite like talking to the people involved in person for getting the feel of a case.

A short while later, I was just checking my email when I noticed one headed "Clive Pettit" our director. I debated for a moment or two whether to open it or just ignore it, but eventually deciding that it is better to know the worst, I opened it. As I had thought, it was about the casting for the next CAOS extravaganza, *The Gondoliers*, although I was slightly surprised that it was a personal email to me, and not a general round robin one.

My Dear Ben, it began,

Thank you so much for attending the auditions for our forthcoming production of The Gondoliers. As always, you gave your all to your performance, and I am delighted to tell you that you have been selected. The role is, I think, well suited to your talents and I know I can rely on you to bring your dedication and, if I may say so, professionalism to the performance.

I am enclosing a full list of the proposed cast and schedule of rehearsal times.

I look forward to working with you once again,

Yours

Clive Pettit

Director, CAOS

I felt a momentary thrill of excitement and was just about to check out exactly which part I had been given when the phone buzzed. It was Janet.

'Mrs Thurstan is in reception for you.'

'I wasn't expecting her yet,' I replied in some surprise. 'I thought you were going to make an appointment for tomorrow?'

'I did,' Janet snapped back, 'but she says she was just passing by this way and thought she would like to get it over with.'

'OK, Janet,' I said, 'just give me a couple of secs, then show her in.'

I hastily picked up the relevant files, a notepad and a pen, and went over to the other side of my office, which is furnished with soft leather sofas and a low table, to lend a more relaxed air to my meetings. A peremptory knock on my already open door announced the arrival of Janet and my visitor and I stood up as they entered.

'Mrs Thurstan for you,' Janet murmured, and as she left the room, I got the distinct impression she gave me a wink.

I used to be a great fan of Sir Arthur Conan-Doyle's *Sherlock Holmes* stories, and I remember in particular the one entitled "A Scandal in Bohemia" in which we were introduced to Irene Adler, thereafter referred to by Holmes as "*the woman*". When relating these events to Marcus later, I used the same expression about Rosamund Thurstan, qualifying it only by adding "apart from Julia".

Rosamund Thurstan floated into my office borne, it seemed, on a wave of delicate perfume and an almost tangible golden aura. She was tall and slender, with shoulder length blonde hair and a skin of iridescent silkiness. Her hand touched mine with the sensation like the stroke of a butterfly wing and her long fingers caressed my palm as she withdrew sending a distinct tingle down my spine. Her voice was low and soft, like the breeze across a field of wheat.

I motioned her to a seat, and she sat, crossing one elegant leg over the other, then looking directly into my eyes breathed, 'It's so good of you to look after me, Mr Jonson.'

'Oh, please call me B-B-Ben,' I stammered and felt myself flushing like a hormonal adolescent.

'And I'm Ros.'

There was a slight pause as I endeavoured to pull myself together and get my brain into gear. I noticed Ros' eyes flash around the room and settle on the photograph of me, Julia and the children which stood on a low table. She did not say anything, but the slight inclination of her head prompted me to reply to the unspoken question.

'My wife and children,' I confirmed.

She intoned, 'How lovely.'

I cleared my throat. 'Right, well, let's get down to the business in hand…er…Ros,' I began, 'I gather from the notes I've seen that you think your husband is not being entirely straightforward in his declaration of assets and income?'

'You could put it like that,' Ros looked at me with a slightly ironical smile.

'Do you have any evidence of this?' I asked.

Ros considered for a moment before replying. 'Well, I'm sure that the value of the company has been deliberately held down for one thing,' she began.

'Yes, we're looking into that,' I replied.

Ros nodded, then went on, 'And I have a feeling he's been hiding money somewhere. But I have no proof.' She looked at me helplessly.

'So Garnet's not such a gem, then?' I said, trying to inject a little levity.

Whatever Ros Thurstan's other attributes were, a sense of humour was not amongst them, as she looked at me blankly.

We talked at some length on her own position and such assets which she knew about. I asked about her husband's current spending habits, as far as she knew, and it certainly seemed clear that his expenditure far exceeded his declared income. Ros herself had been obliged to find employment again as the money from Thurstans dried up, and although still living in the rather splendid marital home, she struggled to make ends meet.

'Garnet's supposed to pay all the bills for the house,' Ros looked tearful, 'but he often doesn't, and I get the threatening letters, so I end up paying. So what with the stress of him going and a bereavement as well, I'm at my wit's end.'

I looked duly sympathetic. 'Well, we will see what we can do, Ros,' I finished, 'I'll be in touch.'

'Thank you, Ben, you've been so kind,' she breathed as she took my hand on her way out of the room.

For a brief moment, she leaned forward as if to kiss me, then thought better of it and moved away, leaving my heart pounding.

I couldn't help watching her from the door of my office as she walked away down the corridor with an elegant yet purposeful stride and was slightly discomfited when she half-turned and gave a little wave, as if she had sensed my eyes on her. I was more discomfited still when I turned around to find myself face to face with Janet, who had arrived silently behind me.

'You've been so kind, Ben,' Janet intoned in a ruthless parody of Ros' husky tones, then went on in her normal more gravelly tone, 'Quite something, isn't she?'

'Mrs Thurstan is a very pleasant lady who has been treated badly by her husband and I am anxious that this firm does its utmost to assist her,' I retorted, feeling the colour rising in my cheeks once again.

Janet gave me a knowing look. 'Have you had the cast list from Clive yet?' she asked, and I was relieved by the change of subject.

'Oh, yes, I have. I was just going to look at it when Mrs Thurstan arrived,' I said, moving over to my desk and sitting down in front of the screen.

'I'll leave you to it then,' Janet gave me another strange look as she left the room.

I looked at the list Clive had sent me. I noted that Randall had indeed been cast as Marco, but that was not a surprise. I read further down the list. Not the Duke – well, no surprise again there. Not Luiz either, nor Guiseppe, nor Antonio. I finally found my name against the character of Francesco. I quickly looked up the role.

The character sketch stated simply: "Francesco: The youngest of the Venetian Gondoliers we meet and a member of the chorus."

I felt somewhat deflated and scrolled through the libretto to see exactly was involved and found, as I had begun to suspect, that it was not much. I was beginning to think that it was hardly worth the effort…

A couple of weeks passed. I had initially considered declining the part of Francesco and standing on my dignity. I had discussed this with Marcus that evening as we sat around the breakfast bar in the kitchen, nursing a glass of wine.

'Oh, don't be such an ass!' he had exclaimed. 'At least you're in the production, with a named part. And anyway, it says he's the youngest of the gondoliers, so that's actually quite flattering.'

'You haven't seen the other gondoliers,' I remarked dryly.

He had gone on to point out that the character sketch notes referred to the Duchess, the part Janet was to play as "The wife of the Duke of Plaza Toro. A contralto battle-axe in the classic G&S style."

'A veritable triumph of type-casting!' he had laughed.

But I had decided Marcus was right and swallowed my pride. Rehearsals were due to start the following evening and I busied myself learning the songs. In the meantime, work had progressed on the Thurstan case. We had prepared a report on the valuation of the company, Thurstans Limited, which made interesting reading. The fortunes of the company had indeed appeared to take a dive, coincidentally or otherwise, around the same time that Garnet Thurstan and the lovely Kelsey were getting together, so to speak. There seemed to have been a number of slightly unusual transactions involving property and bank deposits, with the result that the net assets of the company were seriously depleted over a couple of years. The trading side did not seem to be so affected, although again, mysteriously and perhaps coincidentally, the profitability of the company had plummeted. On the basis of the reported figures, as I said over the phone to Tom Bremner one afternoon, we could not disagree markedly with the company valuation that Garnet Thurstan's solicitors had produced.

'The point though, Tom,' I said, 'is what was the reason for this sudden change? It looks to me as though there has been a deliberate attempt to shift value out of the company.'

'How has Thurstan done that?' Tom asked.

'Well, there are a number of ways,' I replied, 'A profitable business can have bad years: with the art of creative accounting, suddenly there are write-offs or investments that were never mentioned before. You can use false business transactions – paying off a debt that was never a debt to a friend's company, while that friend holds the money on trust. Or ghost-invoicing – paying for things that aren't real. Or false litigation claims where your friend or colleague pretends to be in a dispute with you. Or paying rent that isn't real rent. It's money-laundering, effectively.'

'Can we prove any of this?'

I sighed. 'It's a bit difficult without any clues as to where the money has gone. I'll try talking to Ros, I mean Mrs Thurstan, again to see if she can come up with anything. As a last resort, could we apply to the court for power to look at Garnet Thurstan's computer and other records?'

Tom clicked his tongue in irritation. 'Well, we could possibly. But it is very much a last resort and we'd need to convince the court that there is strong circumstantial evidence that Thurstan is doing something dodgy. The courts don't like us just going in on a fishing exercise.'

'OK, well, I'll see what we can do,' I promised and rang off.

I asked Janet to get hold of Ros Thurstan again but she was not answering. I decided to go and have a look at Thurstans' premises for myself, mainly to get a flavour of the outfit, though sometimes one can learn something useful.

I walked the three hundred yards back home and retrieved my car from the garage, then drove the twenty miles or so to the dismal, windswept trading estate where Thurstans Limited had its headquarters. I had to think of some excuse for going in to the office of the company, as I clearly did not want to announce myself and say I was here to see if the books were being cooked. I decided that a reasonable strategy would be to ask for directions to some other business on the industrial park.

So before going to Thurstans, I drove around a while and made a note of one I found in a remote corner of the estate, the rather incongruously named Pacific Engineering Company Limited. Thus armed, I drove on and turned in to the car park of Thurstans.

I pulled into a parking bay marked "Visitor" and climbed out of the car. I took a good look around the forecourt of the building, and noted another bay marked "G Thurstan" which housed a fairly non-descript looking Ford.

At least he's got the sense not to show off by keeping a fancy motor, I thought.

Over on the far side though was an altogether different machine: a dark blue Bentley with a personalised number plate. Mentally noting that, I pushed open the door of the office and entered the reception area. There was no one at the desk, but a sign said "Please ring for attention" above a small button. I duly pressed this and a few seconds later, I heard the sound of high heels coming towards me and a pleasant-faced young woman appeared. I was interested to read her security badge, which displayed the name "Kelsey Nelson".

Not in the same league of sexual attractiveness as the sultry Mrs Rosamund Thurstan, I thought.

'Can I help you?' Kelsey asked.

I explained I was seeking the premises of Pacific Engineering. Kelsey looked mildly surprised, 'Not been asked that before,' she began. 'Not sure actually. Didn't your sat-nav tell you?'

I had already prepared for this one. 'I've only got the postcode address and it doesn't seem to get me to the right place.'

'Oh, yes, I see.' She seemed satisfied with that answer. 'Well, I'll have to ask someone. Oh here you are, here's Mr Thurstan, he'll know.' She turned to address a rather bulky man with a red complexion and a mane of thick grey hair, who was heading in our direction.

'Garnet, this man here,' she gestured in my direction, 'is looking for Pacific Engineering. Do you know where it is?'

Garnet looked towards me. 'Pacific Engineering? What would you want with them?'

'I'm afraid I couldn't tell you, it's a confidential matter,' I replied smoothly, with an apologetic smile. 'Do you know where I can find them?'

'Down the road, turn left then second right. I think it's called Norwood Way,' Garnet replied. 'Excuse me, I've someone waiting for me.' He turned to Kelsey, saying 'Could you organise some coffee for us please, Kels?' then hurried away.

'Thanks, Mr Thurstan,' I called after him, and he waved a hand in acknowledgement. I looked back to Kelsey.

'Thanks for your help.' I went to leave, then a thought struck me.

'Nice Bentley in the car park,' I said to Kelsey. 'Is it the boss's?'

She shook her head. 'No, no. That belongs to Mr Thurstan's visitor. A customer.'

I nodded. 'Right. OK, well, thanks again. I'd better get on my way.'

I headed back to my car and set off in the direction indicated by Garnet Thurstan. But once out of sight, I altered course and headed for the office. The visit had not produced anything especially revelatory, but it was interesting to meet the other main characters in the drama, as it were, and get a feel for Thurstans itself. I did though have one or two ideas which I needed to follow up...

The next evening was the first rehearsal of *The Gondoliers* and I duly turned up at the church hall at six-thirty. I had not progressed much further with the Thurstan case, as Ros Thurstan had been unable to see me, though she had promised to call in at my office the following afternoon after she had finished work.

The evening started smoothly enough, although I was perhaps not the only one to be mildly irked by the way Clive fawned over the new recruit.

'Oh, wonderful, Randall, you've caught it nicely,' he kept saying, 'Look, everyone, just see what Randall is doing here!'

After an hour or so of this, the Duke of Plaza Toro had evidently had enough, for he turned to me and said, not so *sotto voce,* 'Bugger Randall, I'm going to the pub!' and walked off.

Worse was to come, for Randall, having got his feet beneath the table as it were, proceeded to interrupt proceedings with helpful suggestions.

'Sorry, Clive, if I may? Don't you think it would be better if Guiseppe at this point did this?' and demonstrated some little routine.

Clive was still in thrall to the young *arriviste* and eagerly seized on these pointers.

'Oh, yes, splendid, thank you, Randall.'

I was not immune from the helpful Randall, even though my part was, not to put too fine a point on it, miniscule.

Virtually my only solo line went:

'Good morrow, pretty maids;
for whom prepare ye
These floral tributes extraordinary?'

And after I sang these, Randall stopped the ensemble and said, 'I don't like to be picky, Ben, but don't you think the emphasis should be more like this, then proceeded to sing the lines in a manner which, to my ear, sounded remarkably like the way I had just done it. Clive again responded enthusiastically in support, so I bit my tongue and meekly agreed.

I was glad when the evening finished and I could head home, though at the same time wondering how I could cope with another three months of rehearsals…

The next morning saw me back at my desk, when Janet bounded in to my room.

'To free you from all encumbers, leave it to us to do the numbers,' she announced triumphantly.

I lowered the file I was reading. 'I beg your pardon?'

I looked over my glasses at her.

'The slogan. What do you think?'

I put the file down on my desk. 'What I think, Janet, I would hesitate to put into words.'

'You don't like it then?' she glared at me.

'I think you could safely infer that,' I replied. And before she could reply, continued, 'Look, as I've said before, let's leave it to the experts, should we?'

'Well, tell the experts to get a move on then,' Janet retorted.

Although irritated, I thought it best to change the subject, so I quickly said, 'How did you think the rehearsal went yesterday?'

Janet's face at once lit up. 'Oh, brilliantly. Randall is such an asset to the company, isn't he?'

'Not sure if the "Duke" would agree with you there,' I said, 'he disappeared fairly smartly.'

Janet's lips tightened. 'Oh, he's just an old soak. Can't wait to get to the pub every night.'

I let the subject drop and Janet went off.

The day passed quickly and I soon found it was time for my appointment with the luscious Ros Thurstan. Sure enough, she arrived promptly and was ushered into my office.

She was wearing a rather low-cut top and I had difficulty dragging my eyes away from her cleavage.

'Well, Ros, I just wanted to keep you abreast of things...er...I mean keep you up to date,' I began.

'Thank you, Ben,' the soft, husky tone sent shivers down my spine once more. 'Oh, and you asked about friends of Garnet's who might possibly have helped him to conceal things?'

I nodded.

'Well, there is one I think who could have done. His name's Alan Parrish and he's got various businesses. He and Garnet have known each other for years and used to meet almost every week.'

'Alan Parrish, you say?' Something rang a bell there. 'He doesn't drive a Bentley, does he?'

Ros considered. 'I'm not sure. I don't really notice cars. But he could do. Why?'

I was fairly sure we were on to something here. The registration of the car I had seen at Thurstan's had contained the initials "AP" but I did not want to admit to Ros that I had been to the factory.

'Oh, no particular reason,' I said casually, 'OK, we'll investigate this guy.'

'And there was one other thing,' Ros leaned forward towards me and the low-cut blouse went lower still, so that I had hurriedly to avert my eyes. 'I remember Garnet talking on the phone to someone about the "New China Bank", but I don't think we ever had an account there. Perhaps it means something?'

I made a note of this too. I brought her up to date with our report on the company and the suspicion that there had been some dodgy dealing. I went on to say that if we could not find any evidence, we might have to get a court order to look at Garnet's private records, including his computers.

'Oh, don't do that,' Ros immediately looked alarmed.

'Well, it's very much a last resort,' I replied, 'but why shouldn't we?'

'Oh, it's just that I wouldn't quite like that. I'd rather we came to some amicable agreement.' I must have looked a bit doubtful at this, as she hurriedly went on, 'I mean he is still the father of my children. I don't want there to be too much ill-feeling.'

I nodded. 'Yes, well, let's hope we can avoid going down that route.'

She left soon after and again made as if to kiss me, but changed direction at the last moment. And again, as I watched her float down the hallway I was surprised by Janet appearing from behind me. I wasn't entirely comfortable with the look of suppressed amusement with which she regarded me.

To cover my discomfort, I issued some instructions to her and then settled back to think. I looked through the report on Thurstans and sure enough, there seemed to have been a disposal of property in the previous year. And by all accounts, the company had some fairly hefty lease agreements.

It seemed probable that Garnet had sold the premises I had visited and then entered into a leaseback agreement. And again probable, in the circumstances, that he had sold them at an undervalue to a friend, with the intention of buying them back again once the divorce was out of the way.

It was also highly likely that the rent agreement for the same premises had been set pretty high as a way of getting profits out of the company. Presumably these also could be clawed back at some future date. I had asked Janet to investigate Alan Parrish's businesses to see what we could turn up. It was a bit of a long shot but worth a try. If we found nothing, we would have to consider going to court to get hold of Garnet's computers. I wondered again why Ros had been so reluctant for us to do that.

Then there was the New China Bank angle as well. This might prove more difficult, though if I got Tom Bremner's firm to ask them for information, there was a chance that something may be revealed. I rang Tom and asked him to see what he could do.

I checked my emails and was surprised to see one from Clive, asking if we could all come for a further rehearsal that evening.

Bit short notice, I thought, somewhat indignant, but as Marcus was away, I replied that I would be there.

An hour or so later, Janet put her head round my door and reminded me about it.

'I'm off now,' she said. 'Will you be long?'

I grunted. I was in the middle of a report that I had promised Tom would be ready for the next day, so I wanted to complete it before I left.

'I'll be there as soon as I can,' I replied shortly. 'But Clive has to remember that most of us have work to do.'

'Well, I think it was actually Randall's idea,' Janet said, to my surprise, 'Clive rang me earlier about something else and mentioned that Randall had some ideas for the group.'

'Oh, good! How thoughtful of him!' I said, in a sarcastic tone.

'Yes, isn't it? I knew Randall would be a good addition to the society,' came the reply.

Sometimes I think irony is wasted on her.

It was after seven by the time I had finished. I locked up then sprinted along the high street to the church hall. I pushed open the door and was nearly knocked to the ground by the burly figure of the "Duke" heading in the opposite direction, muttering obscenities under his breath. Inside the hall was a scene of some disorder. There was a babble of voices and I found the cast and chorus standing in a rough circle, talking to each other, whilst Clive was in the middle, clapping his hands and trying to attract attention. Randall was at the far end of the room, sitting on a chair and holding his stomach, with Janet and one or two other female members of the chorus fussing over him.

'What the hell's going on here?' I muttered to "Guiseppe" who was standing on the side-lines, and to my surprise, idly bouncing a large ball up and down on the ground.

'Oh, you've missed a real treat,' he replied with a grin, 'Randall over there decided we needed to make the rehearsals more stimulating. And so he suggested to Clive that we start off with what he called "a sprint rehearsal".'

'What on earth's that?' I asked in astonishment.

'Well, it's a run through the scene line by line, apparently. The cast stand in a big circle and run through the lines as quickly as possible. No pauses, no drama, no emotion, just raw speed.'

'Well, I'm not entirely sure I see the point, but it doesn't sound too bad' I replied.

'Oh, that bit went quite well,' Guiseppe replied, airily, still bouncing the ball, 'it was the next part that caused the trouble. Randall then suggested we introduce this rubber ball,' he gave the ball an extra hard bounce to demonstrate, 'whatever character is speaking holds the ball in his or her hands. At the end of their line, they toss the ball to the next speaker and so on. The idea is to use the physical act of throwing the ball to mirror the emotional act of the line. If the character is angry, they'll throw it with some intensity. If the character is loving, they'll toss it gently and so on.'

A suspicion was beginning to form in my mind.

'Don't tell me. The Duke…?'

'Spot on!' Guiseppe grinned broadly once more. 'The "Duke" was getting more and more impatient and kept throwing the ball harder and harder. When Randall stopped proceedings and said to him, "I think the Duke is quite happy at this point, you know," the 'Duke replied, "No, he isn't. He's bloody p****d off with this b******s," and hurled the ball right into Randall's stomach. Randall went down like a ninepin, the girls all rushed round him, Clive started flapping about like a demented chicken and the "Duke" marched out saying "I'm off to the pub".'

'Oh dear.' I tried to suppress a grin, but failed utterly and Guiseppe and I started laughing uncontrollably.

Unfortunately, Janet came over at this point and gave us a look of some disfavour.

'Well, I'm glad you two find it funny,' she snarled. 'Poor Randall could have been seriously injured.'

'Oh come off it, Janet,' Guiseppe responded, his laughter having suddenly subsided. 'The only thing that was hurt was his dignity. Come on, Ben, I think the "Duke" has the right idea. Let's go to the pub.'

'Perhaps another time,' I said, as Janet fixed me with a glare.

The room was still in something of a state of turmoil so I went to the middle of the circle and clapping my hands loudly, I called everyone to attention. Gradually, the noise died down, and I handed over to Clive, who in a state of some distraction said, 'Well, ladies and gentlemen, perhaps we should leave it there for this evening and reconvene next week. Thank you very much.'

We all shuffled out of the hall and I made my way back home. I had barely opened the door when my phone rang. It was Tom.

'Sounds as though you had a lively time tonight, old boy,' he boomed as I found a stool and sat down. 'More like the Grenadiers than *The Gondoliers*!'

'Ah! You've heard about it then?'

'Of course! Your colleagues – who are they? – the "Duke" and Guiseppe? – came in and could talk of nothing else. Best laugh I've had all day!'

'Yes, I'm sorry I missed most of it,' I said.

'Actually, I wanted to speak to you about something else,' Tom went on in a confidential tone.

'Oh yes?' I replied. 'What was that?'

'That matter we were discussing earlier – the bank query. Actually, they were remarkably helpful when I explained the circumstances. They're sending me a load of stuff but basically, Garnet Thurstan has deposited the best part of a million with them in the past eighteen months.'

'Mmm, interesting,' I mused. 'Eighteen months, you say? Is that when the account was opened or was it in existence prior to that?'

'No, they said the account was only opened eighteen months ago.'

'Well, good, cheers, Tom,' I poured myself a glass of wine and raised it in salutation. 'Thanks very much.'

A few days passed. My team had beavered away on the Alan Parrish angle and after a bit of digging, they managed to find, as I had suspected, that the Thurstans Ltd premises had indeed been sold at what on the face of it looked like an undervalue to one of Parrish's companies. A leaseback arrangement to Thurstans had also been set up, again, as I had thought, with a rather higher annual rent than was justified. This, coupled with one or two other unusual looking transactions in his companies, gave us enough evidence to bring pressure to bear on Garnet to revise his statement of assets and his advisors to alter substantially their valuation of the company itself. The total increase in Garnet's net worth amounted to some millions, and if as Tom and I anticipated, the divorce settlement split this evenly between Garnet and Ros, then she would end up in a more than comfortable position.

'Very satisfactory, old boy,' Tom bellowed down the phone at me one afternoon. 'Well done! I should think Mrs Thurstan will be very grateful.' I could imagine the big wink with which he said this.

'Yes, I hope so,' I replied, evenly. 'In fact, she's coming in later, so I can let her know.'

'Do we have to report anything to the Inland Revenue or anyone?' Tom asked.

'Well, I don't believe so,' I responded, 'I've rather put the ball in the court of Garnet's own accountants in that regard. I gave them a brief outline of what we had found out so it's up to them to investigate further.'

'Good!' Tom said firmly. 'Perhaps see you later?'

'Well, Marcus is back, but perhaps,' I replied.

Ros Thurstan sipped her tea and listened attentively whilst I explained what we had discovered and the subsequent dramatic improvement in her prospects.

'But that's marvellous, Ben,' she said in her sultry tones.

We were sitting again on the low sofas in my office and she turned so that she closed the gap between us and put one hand on my knee. I let it rest for there for a second, before standing up and moving over to my desk. I felt quite shaky for a moment, but I picked up a file from my desk, then walked back and stood facing her.

'Just a couple of points to clear up, Ros,' I started.

She looked up at me with a slightly puzzled air. 'Yes?'

'Firstly, just as a matter of interest, what subject do you teach?'

She seemed surprised by the question. 'Business studies. To sixth formers generally, but I do some classes at the tertiary college as well.'

I raised an eyebrow. She gave a mirthless laugh.

'Oh, I expect you thought I would be a primary school teacher, didn't you?'

I gave a slight shrug of acquiescence.

'Thought so!' She laughed once more. 'But I'm not just a pretty face, you know.'

'Indeed not,' I confirmed with a nod. 'But moving on, when exactly did Garnet move out of the family home?'

Ros looked uncertain. 'Oh, now let me see, I'm not sure...'

I cut in on her. 'Because according to these notes I've got from your solicitor, it was two years ago last April.'

Ros considered for a moment, then nodded. 'Yes, well, I suppose that must be right. When you're emotionally shattered like I was, time doesn't seem to mean much.' She flashed me a sad smile.

'And you haven't had face to face contact since then?'

'No, I haven't! I couldn't bear to be in the same room as him.' Her nostrils flared.

'That being so...er...Ros, then how come you said you overheard Garnet talking on the phone to the New China

Bank, when that account was only opened eighteen months ago, several months after Garnet left?'

She looked rattled for a moment, but recovering her composure, said smoothly, 'Well, perhaps he had a conversation with them when he was still at home and just thinking about opening an account with them?'

Yes, perhaps,' I agreed and she leaned back in her chair in what seemed to be relief.

'But another thing that puzzled me,' I carried on relentlessly, 'well, two things really. How come you knew about Alan Parrish's involvement for one?'

'Well, I told you, he's an old friend of Garnet's and—'

I interrupted. 'Yes, he is an old friend of Garnet's, but a business friend, and Garnet says that you have never met Parrish. So why did he come to mind?'

'Because I had heard Garnet talk about him.' Ros looked at me with cool detachment.

I conceded the point with a slight bow of the head. 'But the second thing is, why were you so anxious for us not to go after Garnet's computer?'

Ros looked distinctly uneasy now. 'I don't think I was.' She sounded unconvincing.

'Oh, I think you were,' I contradicted her. 'And that together with the fact that you don't teach just business studies, you teach business studies *and* IT made me wonder.'

'Wonder what?'

'Wonder if in fact the source of all your knowledge about Garnet's financial activities was because you had put a keyboard stroke logger on his computers, so that you could find out what he was up to. Read his emails – all sorts of stuff.'

Ros didn't comment for a moment but looked down at her hands, before looking up at me again. 'I think you have an overactive imagination, Ben,' she said in a level tone, then stood up and gazed into my eyes.

I held the gaze for a few seconds. 'Possibly, Ros. But if you had done it, you are aware that it is illegal?'

She didn't comment.

'And there is one final thing,' I said as she started to leave the room. She paused by the door, one hand on the handle, and half turned.

'Yes?'

'Yes,' I replied briskly, 'the bank statements for your joint account with Garnet. We couldn't help noticing the payments going out each month to a certain insurance company.'

Ros shrugged her elegant shoulders. 'So?'

'Well, you see, the payments weren't just for any old insurance policy. They were for an endowment policy. In your name only.'

'Really? Why are you telling me this?'

'Because the policy – or in fact *policies* – are now worth a considerable sum. In fact, around £650,000. And more to the point, you have not included them on *your* statements of assets.'

Ros gave a tinkling laugh. 'Oh, should I have? I didn't realise. And I didn't know they were worth so much.'

'Strange,' I replied, 'because the insurance company confirmed they had provided you with valuations at your request about the time you completed your statement for your solicitor. And then, of course, the bequests – I don't think you've mentioned those either.'

She looked at me for a moment and her hand dropped from the door handle. She came over to me and stood very close. She put one hand on my shoulder and made as if to pull me towards her, murmuring, 'I don't think we need to bother the legal eagles with all that, do we?'

I slid away from her and put out a hand to steady myself. Her gaze went from my eyes down to the photograph on the table I was standing by. She gave a rueful laugh.

'Oh, I see, Ben. Worried about what your wife might think?'

It was my turn to laugh.

'No, I'm not worried about what my *late* wife might think. Not at all. But I do have to consider my current partner.'

'Your current partner?'

'Yes. My current partner. Marcus is his name.'

Ros gave a sharp intake of breath. 'I think I have totally misjudged you, Ben,' she breathed. 'What a pity.'

'Probably,' I replied in a bright tone. 'And should I ring your solicitor to say you're on your way round?'

Ros didn't reply but left the room without looking back.

Janet put her head around the door a few minutes later. 'Your lady friend left in a bit of a hurry, didn't she? Have you two had a lovers' tiff?'

'Yes, thank you Janet, very amusing!' I said sarcastically. 'But in fact, you're not far wrong. If you want to hear all about it, you'd better call Tom and Marcus and get them to meet us at Et Alia in half an hour.'

'Consider it done!' Janet exclaimed, 'I certainly do want to hear what's going on!'

I looked after her as she left. Something had just clicked into place in my mind...

When Janet and I walked into the wine bar, we found Marcus and Tom ensconced in our usual corner. Tom already had a bottle and four glasses and proceeded to fill them up as we sat down and exchanged greetings. I thought that Janet might refuse the wine, but obviously curiosity overcame her moral scruples and she picked up her glass without demur.

Tom was first off. 'OK, young Ben, I think you've got a bit of explaining to do. I've just had my partner on the line telling me that Mrs T has been in to see him in something of a state.'

'Oh, well, that's good,' I replied, 'I did wonder if she might call my bluff.'

I was met with blank looks, so I quickly summarised the recent conversation between Ros Thurstan and I. Marcus looked relieved – I think he gets rather jealous sometimes...

Janet cut in. 'So that was why you asked me to speak to the school and the college about her. To find out what she did?'

'Yes, that's right,' I replied, 'I wanted to see if she was likely to know about these keyboard logging devices and if she had the ability to attach them to Garnet's equipment. It wasn't conclusive, of course, that she taught IT as well, but it was an indicator. And it was interesting that she carefully did not admit it to me.'

'But what made you think of it in the first place' asked Marcus.

'Well, it all seemed a bit too easy for us to find what Garnet was doing. From what I've heard and seen, Garnet is not a fool and he would have been very careful to make sure Ros was not likely to find out. Then the bit about the New China Bank clinched it. I never believed her when she said she had overheard Garnet on the phone, and then when we found out the date the account had actually been opened – months after Garnet had left Ros – well, that sort of confirmed it in my mind. Ros must have had some other source of information.'

Tom interrupted. 'But how did you know about the bequests? Apparently she told my partner that she inherited some property from her father quite recently which she hadn't disclosed to him before. Valuable property, too.'

I grinned. 'That was a lucky guess, really. She had mentioned in one of our meetings that she had been very emotional because of Garnet leaving her and a bereavement, so I just put two and two together. I reckoned that if she was being so devious over these other things, then it was quite possible that if she had inherited recently, she would keep quiet about that too.'

Marcus laughed and ruffled my hair. 'You're a pretty devious so-and-so yourself sometimes, you know, Ben.'

I was about to reply, but Janet leaped in.

'Anyway, now we've got all that sorted out, what about our slogan, Marcus? Ben said you've been working on it.'

'Have I?' Marcus looked blank and I kicked him under the table. He went on,

'Oh, I mean , yes, but it's difficult. I haven't come up with anything yet, but I'm thinking about it.'

Janet gave a sniff as if to say that she wasn't surprised.

I remembered what had struck me earlier.

'But in any case, Janet, you have already come up with the by-line.'

Janet looked startled. 'Me? What was it? Not "Don't waste your time in meditation, We're here to do the calculation" was it?'

I shuddered. 'No, not that. It was what you said earlier, when I asked you to call Tom and Marcus.'

'And that was…?' Marcus queried.

'Janet said "Consider it done". And it's perfect! Exactly what we need. Short, snappy, gives the right vibes.'

I was met with blank looks so I started to explain.

'Look,' I said, 'what do people want when they come to us? They have a problem or they want their accounts prepared or their tax returns sorted out. They're not interested in *how* we do it or probably interested in us at all. They just want us to get on with it and leave them to get on with their lives. So if we say "Consider it done", they should be thrilled.'

Janet considered this for a moment, then nodded in agreement.

'So,' I continued, 'just add that by-line to the letterhead, will you, and the signage?'

'Consider it done!' Janet positively beamed as we all clinked glasses.

Later that evening, after Tom and Janet had made their departures, Marcus and I wended our way along High Street back home. As we walked along in the warm autumn evening, Marcus said, 'I can understand why Garnet was trying to hide stuff from Ros Thurstan, but why did she do all that? I mean the keyboard thing?'

'Well, I think, although I don't know for sure,' I replied, 'that it began some time ago when Ros first started to suspect Garnet was having a fling. I think that after installing the device and having definite proof about Garnet and Kelsey, she tackled him about it, and he was more or less obliged to leave home. Then of course he became very bitter and determined to let Ros have only the minimum he could get away with.'

'Yes, but what about Ros?'

'I'm only guessing, but reading between the lines of what she told me, when she realised the fling was with Kelsey, she got really mad. Because, to be honest, Kelsey is fairly ordinary, certainly not I the same league as the fair Rosamund. So she in her turn wanted to punish Garnet. And then she carried on with the keyboard thing so she could find out what he was up to. Although, of course, she has not admitted any of this.'

'And she even tried it on with you when things got sticky?' Marcus sounded incredulous.

'I don't see what's so odd about that! Some people think I'm not bad looking!' I retorted.

'Me for one, of course,' Marcus said quickly. 'Although it must have been a bit of a shock for her when you said about us!'

I gave a laugh. 'It was quite funny really. Especially for someone like Ros, who is so sure of her power over men.'

'So all in all, a good day's work?'

'Yes,' I replied, 'we've dealt with the Thurstan case and I've managed to satisfy Janet with this blasted slogan she keeps going on about. So there's only one more fly on the horizon, or cloud in the ointment or something.'

And what's that?' asked Marcus.

'Randall Barrett!' I said through gritted teeth, 'he's getting beyond a joke. Something will have to be done!'

4. Ben Jonson and the
Art of Mediation

It was getting on for nine o'clock when I let myself in to my house on Thursday evening. The smell of cooking food wafted from the kitchen as I put down my briefcase and hung up my jacket.

'That smells good!' I remarked, coming up behind Marcus as he stirred the pan on the hob and putting an arm around his waist. 'What's it going to be?'

'Lasagne, of course,' he replied. 'Can't you tell?'

I didn't comment on that. My culinary abilities are strictly limited and I tend to leave that side of things to Marcus, with only the occasional foray into such delicacies as a lightly boiled egg or beans on toast.

'You're late,' Marcus went on. 'Busy day?'

'Well, yes, but I'm not late because of work. I did message you – didn't you see it?'

'Sorry, no, I haven't looked since I got home,' Marcus poured tomatoes into the pan and continued stirring. 'What was it?'

'Bit of a long story,' I said, pouring out two glasses of wine and seating myself on a stool.

It had started about halfway through the afternoon. I was wrestling with a pile of staff appraisals, which I had been putting off going through until Janet, my terrifying office manager, had issued an ultimatum: 'If you don't finish all those this afternoon, I'm going to do them myself!'

As Janet was quite capable of causing a mass resignation of the staff if she were so to do, I sighed and resigned myself to completing the task before close of play.

The phone on my desk suddenly trilled and I picked up the receiver.

'Clive Pettit for you,' Janet said briskly.

This was a bit of a surprise. Clive, our director at CAOS, that is, the County Amateur Operatic Society, was not a regular caller. We have a slightly uncomfortable relationship, for although he had been grateful to me when I was instrumental in clearing his name of an accusation of fraud on a grand scale, my appearances in subsequent G&S operettas which he had produced were, I felt, due more to a sense of obligation on his side than to any appreciation of my talent.

'Clive,' I began, 'this is an unexpected pleasure. What can I do for you?'

'Oh, my dear Ben, yes, how clever of you to know I wanted a favour!' Clive started.

I could see in my mind's eye his hands flying up in his characteristic fashion, and simultaneously thought that it was not clever of me at all, but I let that pass. He went on, 'You see, the thing is…'

'Yes, what is the thing?' I interrupted brightly.

Clive ignored this and carried on.

'The thing is, I've had a note from Derek to say that he can't carry on with the role of the "Duke" and to find someone else.'

Derek Hall was due to perform the role of the Duke of Plaza-Toro in Clive's latest extravaganza, *The Gondoliers*.

'Oh!' I replied, 'that is a bit of a blow. Did he give any reason?'

Clive hesitated. 'No, not really,' he said, 'but between you and me, I think it was because of that…er…incident at the rehearsal the other night.'

'Ah!' I replied.

'Derek was totally out of order, of course,' Clive was sounding aggrieved now, 'and he could have caused Randall a serious injury!'

'Oh, I don't think so, Clive,' I said. 'It was only a plastic ball that Derek threw at Randall.'

Clive snorted. 'Well, be that as it may, the point is, we are in a bit of a fix. The show can't go on without a Duke!'

I began to get interested here. I had, in fact, rather fancied the role of the "Duke" myself, though I had to admit that it would be something of a challenge, as I am really a tenor, whereas part of the Duke is written for a baritone, albeit a comic one. Still, I could be persuaded... 'And you're ringing me to see if I...' I started tentatively.

'Yes, I'm ringing you to see if you can go to Derek and try to persuade him to change his mind.'

My hopes dashed so suddenly and cruelly, I was tempted to hang up there and then, but my better nature took control, and I said, 'What makes you think I can succeed in that?'

'Why, your charm and powers of persuasion, my dear Ben,' Clive responded, adopting an obsequious tone. 'Everybody says you are a natural mediator.'

I was just starting to thaw beneath this warm blast of flattery when he added, 'Besides, you're much nearer his age than the rest of us.'

It was my turn to snort. 'Well, I don't know,' I said,

'"Wherefore waste our elocution

On impossible solution?"'

'Oh, yes, very good,' replied Clive, '*The Gondoliers*. Quite. But there you are, you see. You are obviously the one to have a go.'

I wrestled with my conscience for a moment, but deciding in the end that it was for the greater good of all concerned, I said, 'OK, Clive. I'll speak to him. Do you have his number?'

'Yes, of course,' Clive replied and proceeded to rattle off the digits, which I managed to write down with my left hand. 'But,' he continued, 'better than ringing him, go and beard him in his lair, as it were.'

'And where might his lair be?' I asked.

Clive lowered his voice and said in a confidential tone, 'I think most evenings he can be found propping up the bar at "The Black Horse".'

'Ah!' I replied. The Black Horse was a somewhat downmarket establishment at the other end of the high street, and owing to a rather crudely executed pub sign hanging outside, was locally known as "The Wonky Donkey". Habituees shortened this further and referred to it affectionately as "The Wonk".

I went on, 'Well, The Wonk isn't the sort of place I normally frequent, Clive—'

'Me neither, my dear boy!' Clive interrupted.

'But,' I continued, 'in the interests of peace and harmony, I will sacrifice myself and do as you command!'

'Bless you!' came the grateful response and I could picture in my mind's eye the hands flying up in gratitude.

And so, at the end of the afternoon, I put on my jacket and was just heading for the door of my office when I found Janet barring my way.

'Not off to the wine bar, are you?' she said accusingly, 'because you haven't given me those staff appraisals yet!'

I looked at her coldly. 'Sometimes, Janet,' I said in my most injured tone, 'I think this place is not an office, it's hell with fluorescent lights! No, I am not off to the wine bar, and actually, I have finished those blasted appraisals.'

I picked up a pile of papers from my desk and thrust it into her hands.

Janet merely sniffed and said, 'About time! Well, off you go then,' and turned on her heel.

'Thank you very much, miss,' I called after her, sarcastically.

'Don't mention it,' she replied as she stalked down the corridor without turning her head. Irony is wasted on Janet, as I may have mentioned before. As I followed, it struck me that there was something different about her, though I couldn't quite put my finger on what it was...

I trudged along High Street to my rendezvous, passing as I did so my usual haunt, the wine bar Et Alia next to which was a vacant shop.

Wonder what's going to happen there, I mused as I went along.

The church clock was just chiming six as I pushed open the rather grimy door of The Wonk and entered the saloon. It took a moment for my eyes to become accustomed to the gloom, but I saw that the place was empty apart from a couple of youths half-heartedly playing on a gaming machine in one corner. I crossed the room, pushed open another door labelled "Lounge" and spotted my quarry leaning on the bar with a pint of beer in his hand, talking to a man who I presumed was the landlord.

'Mind if I join you, Derek?' I asked as I slid onto a bar stool alongside him.

He turned in surprise. 'Good Lord! Ben! This is a surprise! Don't often see you in here,' he said.

'No, not often,' I replied, thinking, *Well, actually, never.*

'What are you having?' the landlord asked.

I pointed at Derek's glass and said, 'I'll have a pint of that, please,' as I didn't have a clue what to ask for.

Whilst the landlord was busy, I started on Derek. 'No, I don't often come in here, but I was thirsty and I'd heard you saying they served a decent pint, so I thought I'd give it a whirl.'

I was not entirely sure that Derek believed me, but he nodded affably enough. Just then, the landlord passed me my drink. I reached in my pocket for my wallet, but Derek stopped me.

'No, it's on me. Put it on my tab, Bill, will you?' The landlord nodded and Derek went on, 'Oh, by the way, this is my friend, Bill Wainwright. He owns this place. Bill, this is a fellow member of CAOS, Ben Jonson.'

Bill held out a hand. 'Ben Jonson? The accountant from the high street?'

'That would be me!' I replied, shook hands, then raised my glass in salutation to them both. 'Well, cheers, thanks very much, Derek,' I said and took a sip.

It needed all my self-control not to spit out the noxious fluid, but I managed to swallow a mouthful. Derek was regarding me closely.

'Drop of good stuff, isn't it?' he said. 'Made at one of those micro-breweries down the road.'

"Not travelled well" I was tempted to say, but I kept my counsel and just nodded sagely. We talked about this and that for a few minutes, but eventually I said, 'I heard from someone that you're giving up the part of the "Duke".'

His eyes narrowed. 'Who told you that?'

'Oh, a little bird,' I tapped my nose and laughed knowingly.

'Clive, I suppose then?' he snapped back.

I shrugged. I said, 'What made you resign? You're our stalwart in these shows.'

Derek gave a slight bow of his head in acknowledgement. 'Oh, it was that new guy, what's his name?'

'You mean Randall? Randall Barrett?' I offered.

'That's him. Absolute toss-pot. That rehearsal the other day. Never seen anything like it. And old Clive was lapping it up. Couldn't stand it. I'm not wasting good drinking time standing in a draughty church hall throwing a ball and talking about my motivation. I just want to get on with it.'

I looked at him for a moment. My initial thoughts had been to try to appeal to his better nature to come back into the fold, so to speak, but now I wondered if a different tack might prove more fruitful.

I said, 'Yes, well I know what you mean. You're probably better off out of it. In any case, it has been suggested I take over the part of the Duke. I'm really looking forward to it.'

Derek's jaw fell open. 'You?' he exclaimed. 'You're going to take over *my* part?'

I tried to look modest. 'Well, it has been mooted,' I replied. I didn't add that I was the only one who had mooted it.

'Good God,' Derek went on, 'I don't mean to be rude, Ben, but with the greatest of respect...'

'As someone says when they're about to insult you—' I cut in. Derek ignored the interruption. 'With respect, I'm not sure you would be quite right for the Duke.'

I shrugged. 'Well, perhaps there isn't a lot of choice. And if you have made up your mind to leave…'

Just then, another drinking companion of Derek's bustled up to the bar and Derek's attention turned away from me. I sat sipping the foul beer, wondering how I could get rid of it without causing offence. I felt as though I had probably done enough for the time being to sow some seeds of doubt in the mind of the recalcitrant Derek about his resignation from the show. I was weighing up the possibilities of pouring my drink into the container of a rather moribund pot plant which stood in one corner of the lounge when my reverie was interrupted by my new acquaintance, Bill the landlord.

He leaned on the bar and said in a conspiratorial whisper, 'I am right in thinking that you do all sorts of investigative work on accounts and such?'

I nodded. 'Yes, that's correct. Why do you ask?'

He didn't reply for a moment but looked at my barely touched beer and gave a rueful grin. 'Disgusting, isn't it? Can't stand the stuff myself. Tell you what, let me replace it with something else and if you go over and take a seat at the table in the far corner, I'll join you in a second.'

Somewhat taken aback, I did as I had been bid and walked over to the other side of the lounge. After a short interval, Bill appeared with, to my surprise, two glasses of wine.

'You look like a white wine chap to me,' he said, passing me one of the glasses. 'This is quite a reasonable Albariño that my supplier has in from time to time. See what you make of it.'

My face obviously registered some astonishment that he had that sort of drink in stock, as he laughed and said, 'Oh, I don't bother serving it here. Bit over the top of most of the punters' heads. But I have another business, The Manor House Hotel, which is why I buy in some reasonable plonk.'

I was a bit puzzled. The Manor House Hotel was a rather smart country-house type hotel a few miles out of town, and although not madly expensive, was certainly after a rather different type of clientele than that which habitually graced The Wonk. As if reading my thoughts, Bill started off again.

'Yes, well, The Manor is a bit different from this place. But I wanted to diversify and I came into a bit of money – not enough to buy it outright on my own, but I'm in a sort of syndicate, so we bought it between us.'

'Oh really?' I replied, 'I hadn't heard that. How many of you are there?'

'There's five of us,' Bill said, 'but I've got the largest share, then my cousin has fifteen percent, so between us we have the majority. I oversee the running of the place mainly and my cousin helps out. The others are basically just sleeping partners and don't get involved too much.'

'Do you have a full-time manager there?' I asked.

'Yes, we do, and a deputy. My cousin just comes and covers if there are staff shortages and so on.'

I nodded. 'And I take it there's some problem?'

Bill sighed and nodded ruefully. 'Yes, there is.'

'Takings down, profits down, inventories awry?' I asked.

Bill looked startled. 'How did you know?'

'Ah, well,' I said tapping the side of my nose once more and trying to look mysterious, 'we accountants have our methods!'

'But you're right,' Bill went on, 'that's exactly it. The inventories I can deal with – it's not that much, and I'm used to it from running this place. But the other things – there's something not right. Could you take a look?'

'Well, we can have a go,' I said cheerily, 'but I'll need some info. I'll write down some of the stuff I could do with and perhaps you could get it to me at my office ASAP. We'll take it from there.' I produced a pen and some paper from my pocket, and proceeded to make a list, which I handed over.

Bill seemed happy at this and after a few more minutes' conversation, I left The Wonk giving Derek a cheery wave as I went.

I made my way back up High Street and as I passed Et Alia once more, thought I would put my head in to see if my old chum Tom Bremner was ensconced in his usual place. For once, he was not, so I was just about to go back into the street, when on the far side of the bar, I thought I recognised a familiar face. I swung round again to make sure, but there was no doubt about it. It was Janet, sitting on a bar stool, nursing what looked like a large Pinot Grigio, chatting animatedly to someone with their back toward me. It suddenly struck me what had been different about Janet that afternoon: she was wearing make-up. She must have changed at the office, as the usual severe grey skirt and blouse had been exchanged for a rather daring bright fuchsia cocktail dress.

A sixth sense told me that it was probably advisable not to make my presence known to her, but I was desperate to know who she was with. I quickly hid myself behind a rather generously proportioned chap, who I vaguely recognised as a colleague of Tom's, and peered over his shoulder.

I willed Janet's companion to reveal themselves, so to speak. I did not have to wait long, as he (for it was indeed a man she was with) suddenly swung round on his stool to order more drinks. I gave an involuntary gasp and just managed to duck out of sight before I was spotted, although in the process I became rather too intimately in contact with Tom's colleague who turned and gave me what I can only describe as an old-fashioned look.

I muttered an apology and slunk out of the wine bar with my mind racing…

'And you'll never guess who she was with!'

The lasagne now safely ensconced in the oven, Marcus and I were seated on our own bar stools in the kitchen with a glass of Vino Blanco each, and I was just bringing him up to date with the thrilling events of the evening.

'OK, hit me with it!' he retorted.

'Randall-bloody-Barrett!' I exclaimed with a relish.

Marcus looked suitably surprised.

I went on, 'I mean, he must be at least fifteen years younger than her, for heaven's sake.'

Marcus asked, 'What's this Randall like then? I've never actually clapped eyes on him yet.'

'Oh, well, he's about thirty, six two-ish, dark hair, good-looking, quite muscular…' I trailed off as I saw the look on

Marcus's face. 'And, no, I don't fancy him, thank you very much!' I said firmly.

Sometimes Marcus gets ridiculously jealous, I thought.

Marcus gave a rueful shrug, and said, 'What do you think is going on?'

I thought for a moment. 'I'm not sure anything much, though it is a bit surprising.'

Another thought struck me. 'So that's why she asked me if I was going to the wine bar tonight! I suppose if I'd said "yes", she and old Randy Randall might have gone somewhere else.'

'Like The Wonk perhaps?' Marcus asked with a grin.

I grimaced. 'I can't see either of them in that god-forsaken dump. No, The Manor House might be more their milieu. Which reminds me, I must go and have a prowl round there myself soon and see what's going on…'

Friday morning saw me at my desk early, for once arriving before Janet was ensconced. She appeared in my office after a while, clutching some papers, which looked remarkably like the pile of staff appraisals I had given her the previous afternoon. She started off without preamble.

'I've been through these appraisals and corrected them,' she said, with lips as thin as dental floss.

I leaned back in my chair. 'And good morning to you too, Janet,' I responded crisply. 'But actually, I don't recall asking you to correct them, as you put it.'

Janet sniffed. 'Just as well I did, though,' she retorted, 'some of the things you've put!'

'Such as?' I asked, stung by her insinuation. 'Well, for example, this is what you wrote about Alison in Business Services…'

'Oh, yes, Alice in Ledgerland,' I remarked, recalling her soubriquet.

Janet continued, reading out from the form, '"Works well when under constant supervision and cornered in a trap".'

'I was simply being objective,' I protested.

Janet gave me a look of which Medusa herself might have been envious.

'Or this,' she continued, 'for Alex Crawley—'

'Oh, old "Creepy" Crawley from audit?' I interrupted jovially.

'For Alex Crawley "his staff would follow him anywhere, but only out of morbid curiosity" … "some drink from the fountain of knowledge, but he only gargles". Really!' Janet thumped the file down on my desk.

'Oh, well, perhaps I was getting a bit cross and tired by the time I got to him,' I admitted, 'OK, thank you, Janet, I'll look at those again.'

In an attempt to lighten the mood, I asked, 'Did you have a pleasant evening last night?' forgetting that I was not supposed to know where she had been.

Janet gave me a stony look. 'Yes, thank you,' she said. There was silence for a moment.

'Do anything nice?' I asked encouragingly.

'Yes.'

Another silence.

'And that was…?'

Janet sighed. 'As you very well know, I was having a quiet drink with a friend in Et Alia and we were having a very pleasant discussion until someone came in and made a complete exhibition of themselves!'

I reddened. 'Oh, you saw me then?' I said.

The lips went even thinner. 'We could hardly fail to! What did you do to that poor colleague of Mr Bremner's? He went as red as a beetroot.'

'An unfortunate misunderstanding,' I skirted over the incident, 'So you and Randall were having a good chat?'

Janet nodded. 'Indeed we were. Mainly about the show. Randall said he doesn't think Clive is up to the job as director. And now, of course, Derek's thrown in the towel.'

'Oh, you heard about that?' I asked, surprised.

I thought Clive would have kept that under his hat for a while in the hope that Derek would change his mind.

Janet nodded again. 'Yes, Randall told me.'

I idly wondered how Randall had found out but I let it pass. I was more uneasy about Randall's undermining of Clive, which could throw the whole of the production into disarray.

Another thought struck me and I asked, 'Did you just happen to bump into Randall or was it a pre-arranged rendezvous?'

Janet sniffed and said archly, 'That's for me to know and you to find out!' and left the room.

Really, she can be very annoying at times...

Later that morning, a package arrived on my desk and on opening it, I found a bundle of material which had come from Bill Wainwright, containing financial reports on The Manor House Hotel.

I skimmed through the pile then buzzed one of my assistants to come to my room. We spent some time discussing the case and deciding what we needed to look at. Finally, I packed him off to set to work and made a few notes for myself. In essence, the hotel had been very profitable at the time that Bill and his associates had purchased it, some two and half years previously, though I did wonder why it had in fact been sold at that time.

To begin with, the rate of profit had dipped, not surprisingly on a change of ownership, but although it had recovered somewhat, was still significantly lower than before. The personnel had not changed to any great extent in that time, and as far as I could tell, the systems were pretty much as they had been. I would have to wait for my assistant to run the data through some sophisticated software we use to get more detailed information. But I thought in the meantime it might be as well to go and have a look at the place for myself.

I toyed with the idea of asking Bill to take me round, but he had said he wanted to keep things confidential for the time being, so I decided for the first visit to go incognito, as it were. I quickly emailed Marcus and suggested that instead of an early Friday evening bottle of Vino Collapso at Et Alia we would have a change of venue and see what delights The Manor House could offer us.

I left the office promptly at six and bade a cheery farewell to Janet, who reminded me that there was a rehearsal on Saturday afternoon. Fortunately, Marcus had already arranged a squash game for the same time, so it was not too much of an intrusion into the weekend. I sped along the high street, and finding Marcus already home, we jumped in the car and set off.

The Manor House Hotel was not far away. Our route took us back up the high street, passing The Wonk as we went, then out of town into a maze of country lanes. Finally, we plunged down a narrow road with high hedgerows and trees that met overhead, so it was as though we were driving through a leafy tunnel, until we reached the impressive wrought iron gates of The Manor House and scrunched down the drive before coming to a rest on the gravelled forecourt.

We made our way up the three steps to the imposing front door and entered the hotel. Inside, it was hard at first to make out that this was indeed an hotel and that we had not just stumbled unbidden into the inner sanctum of some wealthy country landowner. But tucked away in one corner of the hall was a reception desk and there were discreet signs on the walls bearing such legends as "Restaurant", "Bar" and "Cloakrooms".

There being no one present at the desk, we walked through to the bar, which comprised two wood-panelled rooms linked by an open archway. The smaller of the two rooms had fitted bookcases rising from floor to ceiling and in the middle of one wall was a handsome fireplace, in which an artfully arranged gas-log fire quietly hissed. There were several people already in occupation and a gentle murmur of conversation greeted us as we made our way to a small table by the window. Nobody remarked our arrival and I went over to the bar and ordered a white wine and a tonic water, which the obliging barman brought over to our table.

I had already briefly outlined to Marcus the reason for our visit but I added some further instructions in a low voice.

111

'Now, what I want you to do, is keep an eye out for any evidence of skimming,' I told him.

'Skimming?' Marcus looked at sea.

'Yes, skimming. It's what we call the little dodges you often get in bars and restaurants. It's known as an "off book" fraud because the cash is stolen before it is entered into the bookkeeping system. It can be the most difficult fraud to detect because there is no direct audit trail that can be followed to the source. Very often, it's discovered by accident, or if someone suspects that it is going on.'

'What am I looking for then?'

'Oh, you know the sort of thing – the barman just pockets the cash for a drink without ringing it up on the till, or doesn't give a receipt – he charges you a fiver for a drink, but only rings up four quid. That sort of thing.'

Marcus looked doubtful but said. 'Well, I'll see what I can do. What are you going to do in the meantime?'

'I'm going to have a prowl round, particularly the bedroom floors and annexe, and see what's what.'

Marcus pulled a face. 'That sounds a bit vague!'

I nodded. 'Well, yes, and probably nothing will turn up. But I like to have a feel for the place and it is amazing what you can find out with just a bit of observation.'

I had a quick swig of tonic-water, then said to Marcus, 'I'm just going to find the cloakroom,' in a voice that was rather louder than was strictly necessary, in case anyone was observing us.

I left him and padded off back to the entrance hall and noting that fortunately there was still nobody at the desk, headed for the stairs to the bedroom floors. I reckoned that if I looked confident enough, no one would challenge my right to be there, but if they did, I would simply say I was looking for the cloakrooms and had lost my way: so sorry.

I made my way down corridors, where most of the doors to the rooms were firmly shut, without meeting anyone. I returned to the entrance and followed the signs for the annexe. This was a fairly recent addition to the building, and comprised some thirty rooms in a two storey building, attached to the old part by a glass walled corridor.

I checked the ground floor, where again all was quiet, except for a cleaning trolley in the corridor and the sounds of a vacuum cleaner in the adjacent room. I thought this was a slightly odd time to be cleaning rooms, but supposed it could have been because of a late check-out by the previous occupant. I made my way up the staircase and had barely reached the top when a door suddenly opened and a figure emerged from a room. We just avoided a collision and I was about to make apologies when I realised who it was. It was Randall Barrett.

'Good heavens!' I exclaimed. 'What are you doing here?'

Randall had an odd look on his face. 'I could ask you the same question,' he replied, for once, his normally urbane manner having slipped somewhat.

I recovered my composure and said playfully, 'Oh, no after you – I was first to ask.'

There was a slight pause, but Randall eventually said, 'I'm staying here for a while. Until I can find a flat.'

It came back to me that Janet had mentioned Randall had only just moved into the area. 'Oh, I see,' I replied, then feeling that I had to add my own explanation, trotted out my pre-rehearsed answer. 'Actually, I'm just here for a drink and was looking for the cloakroom. I seem to have got lost though.'

Randall regarded me dubiously. 'You certainly have. Would you like me to show you the way?'

I could not refuse this offer without arousing suspicion, so I accepted with all due cordiality and followed him down the stairs and back into the main building.

'Just on the left, Ben,' he pointed, before turning and heading for the bar.

I murmured some words of thanks and went into the cloakroom, in case he was watching. I loitered in there for a few minutes, then deciding the coast was probably clear, left and made my way back to the annexe.

I climbed the staircase for a second time and walked down the corridor. Most doors were firmly closed, but one door was ajar and again I noted that the cleaning trolley was outside. I peered through the opening and jumped violently when the door suddenly opened wide and I was confronted by a tall, attractive woman in her thirties, carrying a bucket of cleaning materials.

'Can I help you, sir?' she said.

I thought quickly. 'Oh, yes, I was just looking for a friend, and I thought he said his room was number...er...218,' I replied, having managed to read the number on the door out of the corner of my eye, 'but perhaps I'm wrong?'

'Yes, sir, I'm afraid this room is unoccupied. What was...'

Before I got too entangled in a web of lies, I interrupted and said, 'Don't worry, I'll go and wait for him in the bar,' and hurriedly retreated down the corridor, but not before I had managed to read the cleaner's name-badge. It said "Suzanne Wainwright".

So that must be Bill's cousin, I thought as I retraced my footsteps once more. I had just assumed the cousin was male, but there was no real reason to make that supposition. And Bill had said that the cousin helped out in the hotel, although again, I had rather thought it would have been more in a managerial capacity than a physical one.

My peripatetic ventures had not turned up anything startling, but they had given me one or two ideas...

I entered the bar once more and saw that Marcus had vacated the table we had originally occupied. I wandered through to the adjoining, rather larger, room, which had evidently once been the drawing-room of The Manor House and was now furnished with soft sofas and low tables in a discreetly tasteful, if anonymous, style. I espied Marcus, seated on one such sofa, talking animatedly to another man, who, although his back was toward me, I immediately recognised as Randall.

I heard Randall saying, 'Well, Marcus, if you can't beat them...'

Marcus interrupted and said, 'No, Randall, I know some people say "If you can't beat them, join them". I say "If you can't beat them, beat them", because they will be expecting you to join them, and so you will have the element of surprise!' He laughed at his own witticism, whilst Randall merely looked mystified.

He had been speaking in a rather thick tone and I wondered how many glasses he had downed in the time I had been away.

He looked up as I approached and said, 'Oh, hi, Ben. We were just talking about the G&S group and the good Doctor here was saying I should join the company.'

'The good doctor?' I asked puzzled.

Marcus looked impatient. 'Yes, yes, Randall here is a GP. He's just joined that practice on the other side of town.'

'Oh, I didn't realise,' I replied lightly, 'Congratulations Dr Barrett. I suppose the surgery isn't in Wimpole Street, is it?' My literary allusions were obviously completed wasted on my audience as they both looked at me blankly.

'No, King Street,' Randall replied matter-of-factly.

I became aware that Marcus was leaning towards Randall and running his hand around the collar of his open-neck shirt, revealing rather more chest hair than was strictly appropriate. There was no doubt about it, Marcus was flirting with Randall. For his part, Randall seemed entirely at ease, though whether this was because he welcomed the attention or had simply not noticed, was hard to tell.

'Come on, Marcus, time we were off,' I said, with a slightly harder edge to my voice than I had intended.

He must have realised, because he looked momentarily surprised and I thought for a second he was going to refuse. But he nodded and heaved himself up from the sofa. Randall too stood. We shook hands and made our farewells. Randall, I thought, didn't look too distraught at our departure.

In the car on the way home, Marcus was extolling the virtues of Randall. 'Very charming, isn't he? You didn't say that about him, Ben. And quite good-looking, I have to say…'

It was all uncannily reminiscent of the reaction from Janet on meeting the blasted man, I thought.

I finally exploded. 'Quite good-looking? You practically had your tongue down his throat, for God's sake!'

'Don't be absurd!' Marcus relapsed into a sulky silence.

Supper was eaten in a strained atmosphere. Perhaps I had lashed out too hastily, but I was not yet quite ready to apologise. It was uncomfortable to think that I could have such feelings of jealousy...

In an effort to make conversation, I asked Marcus if he had seen any evidence of skimming whilst I had been otherwise occupied.

'Difficult to say,' he replied, still a little coolly, 'but when I asked for a receipt for the drinks, they didn't look entirely pleased.'

Oh well, I thought, *we will have to send in the troops to investigate further.*

The next morning, I stiffened my resolve and made a fulsome apology to Marcus for my remarks the previous evening. He had the grace to accept this and in his turn apologise. Normal relations having been established, we went our separate ways that afternoon, he to his squash match whilst I sauntered up the high street to the church hall.

There was a noticeable frisson in the atmosphere as I pushed open the door of the church hall. The cast were wandering around and stopping from time to time, without speaking, whilst our director, Clive was standing in the middle of the room, wringing his hands and in deep discussion with Janet. He looked up as I approached and for once looked positively pleased to see me.

'Oh, dear Ben, have you any news for me?'

I replied that Derek, aka the Duke of Plaza-Toro, had not actually agreed to return and saw that Clive looked disappointed. 'Just give Derek a few days, Clive,' I tried to reassure him, 'I think he'll come round eventually.'

'Why would he?' Clive asked.

I explained that I had suggested to him that I would take over the role myself.

Clive and Janet both looked at me in a way that I can only describe as aghast.

'Well, I don't think it's such a bad idea,' I replied, rather nettled, 'but in any case, it's only a ruse to get Derek back.'

They both seemed a bit uncertain about this, but Clive finally nodded. 'Well, my dear Ben, I suppose it's worth a go.'

In an effort to change the subject, I asked, 'Anyway, what were you two talking about? You both seemed very earnest.'

Janet spoke before Clive could reply. 'I was just suggesting to Clive some ways to make the rehearsals more productive,' she said in a firm tone. 'A couple of ideas Randall had.'

'Oh yes?' I replied, 'actually, where is Randall? I haven't seen him here.'

'He's held up,' Janet said. 'He's been on call this morning and it's overrunning. He should be here soon.'

You seem very well informed, I thought to myself, *obviously you and Randall are in frequent communication.*

Out loud I said, 'Oh, right. But what suggestions?'

Janet took up the baton with enthusiasm. 'Well, there are so many really. Randall is so good with these things, but the one we've already started with was what he calls The Random Walk.'

I looked at her blankly. Janet went on with exaggerated patience, 'What we do is ask the actors to walk around the room and stop by someone without saying anything, then take both their hands and look into their faces, still without speaking. The idea is to improve focus and establish a close relationship with other members of the group.'

Clive looks less than impressed with this idea, I thought.

I tried to appear non-committal, so nodded and said, 'I see. And that's what they're all doing now?'

Janet agreed enthusiastically. 'That's right. I really think it's working.'

'What else is on the menu then?'

'It's what Randall calls "Musical Meditation". Firstly, we provide Betty, our accompanist, with some music of varying tempos. Then the actors spread out across the room and hold their hands in the air, whilst moving to the rhythm of the music and feeling how it affects them. After we have done this for a few minutes, the director or someone calls out a mood, such as "happy" or "sad" or "angry" and we all have to try to show that emotion through our movements.'

Clive and I looked at each other dubiously, but Janet had got the bit between her teeth and clapped her hands loudly to attract everyone's attention. She outlined the next phase in the rehearsal process.

The reaction was undoubtedly mixed, with attitudes falling more or less along gender lines. On the whole, the girls were sympathetic and set to with enthusiasm, whilst the men looked sullen. I was loitering on the side-lines, thinking that this was all ridiculous, but at the same time, trying to avoid a direct confrontation with Janet.

I wondered that Janet could be so much in thrall to Randall. It struck me that she had a "thing" for him, hence the make-up and the frock the other night. What Randall was doing wooing Janet was altogether beyond me. As I had pointed out to Marcus, Janet must be at least fifteen years older and not exactly a beauty. Was he just trying to cause mayhem or…?

At this point, the man himself walked in and as he strode up the hall, another thought struck me. Randall was just so totally self-obsessed that he didn't consider the effects of what he was doing. That he was vain, I was in no doubt. The carefully trimmed hair and beard, the clothes he wore and his whole demeanour made that clear. He had no doubts about his attractiveness to either sex, I realised, and he used this fact, if not deliberately, then at least without thought for the consequences.

Before he could speak, there seemed to be a commotion in the "Musical Meditation" group in front of us. A number of the men, having seen Randall enter, started to vent their irritation on him and the rehearsal broke up in some disorder.

Shouts of "waste of time" and "plonker" could be clearly heard. Randall looked bemused, and Clive somewhat out of his depth, so I quickly went to the middle of the room and clapped my hands, indicated to Betty to cease tinkling away, and called for order.

'Right, now that we've warmed up, so to speak,' I went, 'we'll get on with the main rehearsal. Clive, do you want to take the lead?'

Clive looked at me gratefully then putting his rather podgy hands together said, 'Yes. Thank you, girls and boys, if we can now move on. We'll take it from the top and as Derek can't unfortunately be here today, then Ben here will stand in for him. If that's all right, Ben?' He turned to me.

'Delighted,' I reassured him with a sideways look at Randall and Janet, who both looked somewhat askance.

Fortunately, with only a bit of prompting, I managed to get through the scene without too much problem.

In the break, I noticed Janet and Randall in earnest conversation. I could see from the look in Janet's eyes that she had fallen for Randall's undoubted charms.

Oh dear, I thought to myself, *this is not going to end well.*

Later, I was relaying all this to Marcus over a glass or two of vino veritas and expounding on my theory of Randall's character when it occurred to me that I didn't know how he and Marcus had ended up in conversation with each other.

'Oh, I was just standing at the bar getting a drink when he came up and ordered a glass of merlot, and the barman said "yes, Dr Barrett". Of course, I knew who he must be, so I introduced myself, and it went from there.'

'But I wonder why he was being so chummy with you?' I mused.

'Perhaps he just liked what he saw!' Marcus retorted.

Randall isn't the only one with tendencies to vanity, I thought.

Out loud, I said, 'Perhaps, but I don't think his inclinations are necessarily in that direction, old chap,' at the same time giving Marcus a friendly pat on the shoulder.

Then something else suddenly struck me.

'You know I said I bumped into Randall coming out of a bedroom and that he had a funny look on his face?'

Marcus nodded. I went on, 'Well, I've just realised what the look meant. It wasn't his room he was coming out of!'

Monday morning came round all too soon and I was at my desk early ready for the rigours of a new week. As usual, Janet hove into view before too long, with a face like a proverbial fiddle.

I assumed my best bedside manner and said breezily, 'Good morning Mrs Mathieson, and how are we today?'

I was received with a stony look.

'I couldn't say how you are, but I am perfectly well, thank you,' she said through gritted teeth, 'or at least I was until I started looking at those staff appraisals again.'

'Oh, for heaven's sake, what now?' I cried.

She rifled through a file she was clutching and produced some papers with a flourish.

'Look at these!' she fumed, 'on the staff self-appraisal sections. This man has described himself as a "go-getter" and you've written beside it "Mindlessly wanders around the office every hour or so trying to look busy".'

I shrugged.

'Or this one,' Janet went on ruthlessly, 'he's written "I demonstrate definite qualities of leadership" and you've scrawled "has a loud voice"! And this: "I consider myself highly professional" and you've put "Owns a suit and wears it occasionally". I mean, honestly!'

'All right, all right, I'll alter them!' I gave up the fight. 'Anyway, now you're here, could you ask old Creepy Crawley to pop in, please.'

'If you mean Alex, then yes,' Janet admonished me.

In an effort to deflect her ire, I asked, 'You and Randall seem to be as thick as thieves at the moment.'

Janet looked almost coquettish. 'Yes, well, he does ring me a lot and we have had a few chats about this, that and the other.'

I was tempted to reply, "But probably more this and that than the other," but confined myself to a non-committal 'Oh, that's nice'.

Janet flashed me one of her gimlet looks but left my room without further conversation.

A knock on my already open door a few minutes later heralded the arrival of Alex "Creepy" Crawley himself. To be fair, he is not really creepy, but he is a rather gloomy looking man in his late thirties, with an unfortunate squint, so that I am never entirely sure when he speaks if he is talking to me or something over my shoulder.

'Morning, Alex, come in, come in,' I said cheerily and motioned him to a seat.

'Good morning, Ben,' he replied mournfully, apparently addressing the rubber plant by the window.

'I'm sorry to drag you away from audit today, knowing how fascinating that is,' I said ironically, 'but I have a special assignment I'd like you to tackle ASAP, please.'

I briefly explained about The Manor House Hotel and suggested he went up there that morning to investigate further. I gave him the reports which we had already prepared from the information supplied by Bill Wainwright. 'Should be an interesting change from the usual routine,' I suggested.

'I suppose so,' Alex sighed heavily, focussing on the certificates hanging on the wall to my left. I found myself, as I often do, unconsciously shifting position in my chair in order to be in the centre of his field of vision.

'Good. I've spoken to Bill Wainwright, so he's told the hotel to expect you. The idea is that you are looking at their systems, so we don't alert anyone to Bill's suspicions.'

Alex nodded and stood up.

'Oh, there is one other thing I'd like you to do,' I scribbled a note on a piece of paper and passed it to him. 'It may have nothing to do with our investigation,' I went on, 'But I would just like to know.'

'Of course, Ben,' he said, gazing intently at the waste bin, before he left.

Despite his oddities, and notwithstanding the intemperate comments I had written on his staff appraisal, he did have a good analytical mind and was tenacious in his quest for answers to unresolved questions.

A few days passed. Rehearsals for *The Gondoliers* were still hampered by Derek's absence. Although I felt I was growing into the part of the "Duke" so to speak, I had an inkling others were less convinced. Tensions were becoming more apparent as well within the group between the pro-Randall side (mainly the girls) and the less-than-enthusiastic (mainly the boys). Clive was clearly feeling the strain, and his complexion, which has a vaguely greenish hue at the best of times, was now veering more towards chartreuse than pistachio and he was constantly mopping his brow with a handkerchief. Randall and Janet continued their alliance and it became increasingly obvious that they were having a concerted attempt to undermine Clive's authority, though quite why, I was uncertain.

I was relaying all this to Marcus and my old friend Tom Bremner one night after a particularly fraught session with the ensemble in the church hall. We had repaired to Et Alia for a glass or two of *vin* very *ordinaire* and I was railing against the strain of it all.

I had just returned from a trip to the bar to replenish our glasses when I found Tom and Marcus scribbling away. My heart sank for a moment, because the last time this scene had been played out, the verse that they had written (and I had no doubt that was what they were doing) had been less than flattering as far as I was concerned.

My expression must have registered some disquiet, because they hastily reassured me as I sat down that it was not about me.

'Here,' they said, 'read this!'
'To the tune of "The Duke of Plaza-Toro"
We have got a new recruit, who should be in a garret
He has all the acting skills of a dehydrated carrot
And what is more his voice is like an African grey parrot

122

That narcissistic egotistic quite sadistic Randall Bloody Barrett!'

'Most amusing!' I said primly, 'though in reality, he can actually act and he has a very good voice.'

I do pride myself on trying to be entirely fair to everyone, though I felt impelled to add, 'Blast the man!'

It was a couple of days later when Alex sidled into my office.

'Got a minute, Ben?' he asked, addressing the sofas in the far corner of my room.

'Certainly,' I replied, 'is this about The Manor House?'

He nodded and launched into his report on the findings of our investigations. As we already knew, on the face of it, all the normal financial reports and activity reports did not show any particular problem. Overall occupancy rates were in line, more or less, with the seasonal norms, but in spite of that, total takings were distinctly down. A check on the room rates revealed that these too were in line with the season and if anything, were slightly higher than in previous years.

Alex went on, 'So I did as you suggested.'

'Which was?' I asked.

'I managed to find the daily reports of towels and bedding issues. They are on a separate system, so you can't easily cross-check, but by doing a few tests, I found something interesting.' He produced a file and we poured over the papers together.

'You see here,' he said, 'on certain days, if you compare the numbers of towels and so on issued with the rooms occupied, there is a discrepancy.'

I looked at the page.

'Yes, I see,' I said, 'the number of towels and sheets issued is more than the apparent number of rooms occupied. Which means,' I went on, 'either the laundry or housekeeping have made a mistake or there are additional guests not accounted for.'

'Exactly.' The printer on the side table bore the brunt of Creepy's gaze.

'OK,' I was thinking this through, 'so the obvious way to check would be to see which rooms are occupied and which are not and check that with the main register.'

Creepy nodded. 'Yes, it would be. But of course, we have been looking at past records, not the current register. At the moment, everything tallies.'

'Mmm,' I mused. 'But in any case, if someone is trying to defraud the hotel and they were letting rooms, but keeping the proceeds, which is I assume what we think might be happening...' Creepy nodded in confirmation, 'then the only ways that could be doing this would be either to charge cash, and just pocket the proceeds or somehow divert the credit or debit card funds to a different account from the hotel's bank.'

Again, Creepy nodded in agreement. I continued, 'And in any event, whatever the detail of how it was done, the perpetrator has to be someone with access to the hotels systems and banking. Which makes you think that the most likely culprit is the manager or his deputy. Or perhaps both of them in collusion.'

Creepy didn't respond, but maintained a steady gaze at the filing cabinets.

'OK, Alex, thanks,' I said after a pause, 'I need to look at this in a bit more detail and see where we go from here.'

Creepy turned to go, but I stopped him by asking, 'And that other matter I asked you about. Did you get the answers?'

He didn't speak but pulled out a sheet of paper from the inside of the file and held it out to me. I took it from him and read for a few seconds, then said, 'Thanks again, Alex. Just as I thought.'

I spent the next couple of hours ploughing through the detail of Creepy's investigations. As expected, and indeed as Bill Wainwright himself had indicated, there were some problems with the stocks of drinks, but again as he had said, nothing too serious. That there were inconsistencies in the bar takings was hardly surprising and some of it could be put down to sheer error or carelessness. He had, however, ringed one or two dates where the discrepancies were more pronounced, and I made a note to follow that up further.

But it was the possibility that rooms had been let and the proceeds taken which was the real problem. If it had been going on, as seemed likely, for a while, then the losses could be considerable. No wonder Bill had been concerned. I decided to give him a call and share my findings with him. I put the call through and suggested we have a meeting. As he was short-staffed in The Wonk he invited me down for a drink later in the day.

'I'll open a bottle of Albariño for you,' he promised, 'unless you want to have some more of that special ale?'

I replied and confirmed I would settle for the former, thank you very much, and that I would see him later.

I sped up the high street about five o'clock and once more entered the beer-laden atmosphere of The Wonk. I found Bill again in the lounge bar and he pointed to a table in the corner, saying, 'I'll be right over.'

He was as good as his word and in a few minutes appeared with a glass of wine.

'Not joining me?' I asked.

'No, I'll save it for later when Derek comes in,' he replied.

I quickly outlined what we had discovered so far. When I had finished, he looked at me levelly and said, 'So the 64,000 dollar question is, "Who is doing this?"'

I nodded and replied, 'Of course. There are certain obvious suspects but we need a bit more time to pin it down. Do you want us to carry on?'

'Well, yes,' he replied, slightly surprised, 'that's why I asked you to get involved.'

'OK, then,' I replied, 'I think we will have the answer by the end of the week.'

This was rather more optimistic than the facts warranted but I wanted to make a favourable impression on Bill.

'Oh, and there is one more thing,' I went on, 'I have a little favour to ask you…'

I left the warm fug of The Wonk and headed back along the high street towards the office. I was just debating with myself whether to go back in or have an early shower, so to speak, and head for home instead, when I noticed Janet crossing the road. She did not appear to see me, and although some distance away, I could see that she was wearing *that* frock again. I thought to myself that presumably she was having another assignation with Randall, toyed with the idea of following her into the wine bar, but though better of it and instead resigned myself to a bit more leg-work on "The Manor House Hotel" case.

I'd had an idea which I wanted to explore. Alex "Creepy" Crawley had advised me that the things I wanted to cross-check couldn't be done with the programs we had available, as some of the records were kept in a manual form only. He had, however, extracted some details which I started to look at. I was interested to establish if there was a pattern to the apparent defalcations on the bar takings which may in turn indicate who was responsible.

An hour or so later, I sat back in my chair. It had turned out as I had suspected and there was indeed a correlation. But I needed to do another test, involving a return to The Manor House itself. I wondered about leaving it for the next day, but deciding there was no time like the present, I put a call through to Bill Wainwright and sought his permission for my actions. Although he was surprised when I said what I intended, he readily agreed and I set off for home to collect the car. I felt I could do with some help, but all the staff had left by now, of course, so I called Marcus's mobile.

'I wondered where you were, I was just going to call you!' he cried.

I could hear a lot of background noise, so I asked, 'Where are you? It doesn't sound as if you're at home.'

Marcus laughed. 'No, I'm not. I thought I'd drift down to the wine bar and see if you were here.'

'OK, well, as you see, I'm not,' I replied.

A thought struck me. 'Is Janet in there by any chance?'

'She certainly is,' Marcus said. 'In fact, I'm with her now!'

'Is anyone else there?' I asked, conscious that it was a slightly silly question in a busy wine bar.

Marcus, however, got my drift.

'Not now. Randall was here, but he left half an hour ago. He said he had to cover the "on-call" for the rest of the evening.'

It crossed my mind briefly that perhaps Marcus had not just been seeking my whereabouts, but also that of the rapacious Randall...

'Good!' I responded, brushing such thoughts aside, 'because I could do with some help from both of you. Look, here's what we're going to do...'

Half an hour later, the three of us climbed out of my car and once more went up the stone steps of The Manor House Hotel. The duty manager was at the desk and I announced myself to her. I had asked Bill to organise a report and to leave it for me at reception.

'The name's Jonson, Ben Jonson,' I started, 'I think you have an envelope for me.'

The girl looked at her desk and said, 'Yes, Mr Jonson, that's right. Here you are.'

I thanked her, turned to the others and beckoned them over to a quiet corner.

'Now, here we have a list of all the rooms with the names of the occupants and it also says which rooms are unoccupied and the reason why they're empty.'

'Well, isn't that obvious?' said Marcus impatiently.

'Not necessarily,' I replied. 'Some rooms are out of action for decoration, repair or deep cleaning.'

Marcus looked a bit sceptical, but I went on.

'So, we will divide the list in three and each go and check which rooms are occupied and who's there.'

Janet interrupted, 'But if there is no reply, then we won't know if the room is unoccupied, or the guest is just not in their room.'

'Well spotted!' I said ironically. 'And for that reason, we have our secret weapon – a pass key each.'

I took out of the envelope the keys and gave one to each to Marcus and Janet. 'Now make sure the room is empty before you use this,' I warned them.

'What are we to say if they are occupied,' Marcus asked.

'Oh, just say you are from the management and checking that everything is to their satisfaction,' I said. 'And if anyone complains about anything, I'm sure you can come up with a suitably bland response!'

I divided the report up and handed the sections over. 'Right, you, Janet, take the main house and Marcus and I will tackle the annexe. We'll meet back in the bar when we've finished.'

The others nodded and we set off. I had deliberately sent Janet to an area of the hotel where I did not believe Randall was staying. The consequences of Janet bursting in to Randall's room unannounced did not bear contemplating...

Oddly, though, Randall's name did not appear at all on the list of occupied rooms, a fact which old "Creepy" Crawley had elicited in answer to my written question. In addition, he had found that the room from which Randall had emerged the other evening had been occupied by a single lady. By single, I mean she was the (apparently) sole occupant – her marital status was not specifically recorded. So I had been correct in my surmise...

The check passed smoothly. I knocked on all the doors and entered those where I did not get a reply. The results made for interesting reading. Of the twenty or so rooms on my list, three that were supposedly unoccupied showed evidence of someone present.

I met Marcus in the hallway as I was finishing and we compared notes. He had two discrepancies on his list, so that made five in total. 'And then, of course, there's Janet's section to look at,' Marcus said.

'True, but I wouldn't be surprised to find that everything tallies in the main building,' I replied. 'It would be harder to conceal any hanky-panky there, I would think. Anyway, let's see.'

We hurried across to the bar to find Janet. Just as we were about to enter, she suddenly appeared, dashed passed us, muttering something about needing the ladies and holding a tissue to her face. Marcus and I looked at each other in surprise. I turned to go after her, but Marcus held my arm and said in a low voice, 'Better leave her for a few minutes.'

I turned back, slightly mystified. 'But she looked as if she was crying,' I said, in an awed tone. 'What's all that about?'

Marcus shrugged, said, 'Search me!' and led me into the bar.

We headed towards a quiet corner and sat down at a small table. The bar was quite busy so Marcus volunteered to go to the counter rather than waiting for the barman to come to us.

'Better get a stiff one for Janet,' I said unthinkingly.

Marcus grinned and said, 'Now that could have been better phrased!' and disappeared.

I was looking through the reports when Marcus reappeared with our drinks and put them down on the table. He had a strange look on his face, so I asked, 'What's the matter with you? You look as though you've lost a tenner and found a fiver!'

'It's worse than that,' he said in a low voice. 'Just look who's over there.'

He flicked his head in the direction of the far side of the room. Just behind a pillar, I could see none other than Randall Barrett, talking to a very attractive woman.

'That's strange,' I said, 'I thought he was supposed to be working tonight.'

'That's not the only strange thing,' Marcus said grimly, 'Have you seen who he's with?'

I looked again. 'I don't know,' I said. 'Who is that lady?'

Marcus gave a mirthless laugh.

'To paraphrase an old joke, Ben,' he said, 'That's no lady – that's his wife!'

I walked into my office in a state of apprehension the next morning, wondering how Janet would be. Of course, following Marcus's revelation, it had been easy to understand the cause of Janet's distress the previous evening. Although she made no comment about Randall, we assumed she must have seen him in the bar and gone up to say hello. We could only imagine the embarrassment on both sides when presumably Randall had been obliged to introduce the two women.

We had carefully avoided the subject when she had returned from the cloakroom and discussed our findings in low voices and a business-like way. The journey back to town had been strained, with Marcus and I making bright conversation, whilst Janet had remained tight-lipped and monosyllabic, but I hoped that a night's rest might have had a healing effect.

To the casual eye, Janet appeared much as usual, but I thought I detected slight rings around her eyes and an almost imperceptible tic in her left temple. I made no reference to her erstwhile boyfriend as we discussed the programme for the day.

But as she was about to leave the room, she turned back and said in a quiet voice, 'No fool like an old fool, is there?'

In spite of myself, I felt a lump in the throat and a hot prick of tears in my eyes. I had never before witnessed Janet as anything less than indomitable, and this new side was an uncomfortable revelation. I had not said anything to her about suspecting Randall of dalliance with the woman at the hotel and I saw no point in adding to her discomfort now, although a thought came to me as to how I could put such information to good use...

Although it was tempting to reply to Janet along the lines of "Oh you're not *that* old!", I decided a more sympathetic approach would be wiser. Instead I said, 'You weren't to know, Janet. It was up to Randall to say.'

She nodded and turned away.

I busied myself with summarising the results for the previous night's investigations. As I had surmised, Janet had found no discrepancies in her section of the hotel. This together with my other observations, and the results of the data Creepy and I had looked at, pointed pretty firmly in one direction. I sighed and picked up the phone. Time to call Bill Wainwright once more.

I held the meeting in my office. I decided that it was better on neutral territory and out of earshot of any staff who might be about the hotel. I spoke to all the members of the syndicate which now owned The Manor House without giving too much away, but in the event, it was only Bill and his cousin Suzanne, who arrived.

As I shook hands with Suzanne, she suddenly said, 'Haven't I seen you somewhere before?'

I murmured some bland response, not wishing to draw attention to my somewhat clandestine activities at The Manor House. I motioned my visitors to the low sofas that I have in my meeting area and they sat down. Bill explained that the three missing members of the syndicate had spoken to him and were content to act on his advice.

Suzanne asked, 'What is all this about? Is there some problem with the hotel?'

I cleared my throat, and said, 'Well, yes and no.'

Realising that this was not exactly helpful, I went on, 'The fundamentals of the hotel are fine, but it has been brought to our attention that the financials are not as good as they should be.'

I went on to discuss the problems of the falling profitability and our enquiries into the reasons for this.

Suzanne looked rather annoyed and said to Bill, 'Why didn't you tell me about this? I am a part owner after all.'

Bill shrugged and I interrupted by saying, 'That was mainly my fault. I suggested to Bill that the least said the better, to prevent forewarning any of the staff.'

Suzanne said, 'So let me get this clear. You're saying that there are guests staying at the hotel who aren't registered on the hotel systems, and that the money they are paying for their rooms is going to someone?'

'Exactly!' I said, standing up and pacing the floor. 'And that means it has to be one of the managers who have access to the hotel systems for keys and so on?'

'Precisely.'

Suzanne continued, 'So we better get them in and give them a grilling!'

I stopped my pacing and turned to face her.

'I don't think there's any need for that, is there?' I said evenly. 'Because it was you!'

After the Wainwrights had left, Janet appeared at my desk.

'So what was all that about?' she asked. 'That Suzanne Wainwright didn't look too happy as she went out.'

'No, well, I'm not surprised,' I replied, 'but I tell you what, why don't you join us later at the Et Alia and I'll fill you in.'

'Us?' queried Janet.

'Yes, Marcus will be there, and one or two others. Should be quite a party! But first, I have a little errand to run, so I'll see you over there about six.'

I gave her a mysterious wink, then hurried out of the office and headed for home. Collecting the car, I drove across town and stopped outside The King Street Medical Centre. At the reception desk, I introduced myself and enquired if Dr Barrett were available, muttering something about a message from the Operatic Society. I was instructed to take a seat and after twenty minutes or so, Randall appeared in front of me.

'This is a surprise, Ben,' he said.

From his tone, I surmised it was not an altogether welcome surprise.

'Isn't it?' I said pleasantly, 'Is there somewhere we could talk?'

He looked doubtful for a moment, but then gave a curt nod. I followed him into a vacant consulting room.

'Well?' he asked after shutting the door.

'I just wanted to say that I think Janet was a little surprised to find that you were married,' I said.

He shrugged, 'I don't see why. The subject just never came up, that's all.'

'Oh, I see, of course!' I exclaimed. 'And that probably applied to the lady in room 216 as well, did it?'

His eyes narrowed. 'I don't know what you mean,' he said.

I gave a contemptuous laugh. 'Oh, now come on, Randall, I think you do.'

He looked at me for a second, then said, 'What do you want?'

'Two simple things,' I said lightly. 'Firstly, a bunch of flowers and an apology to Janet wouldn't go amiss.'

He gave another shrug and said, 'That's easy enough, I suppose. What else do you want?'

It was my turn to shrug. 'Well, this bit might be more difficult for you...' I paused for a second and Randall looked at me with a degree of apprehension.

'Yes,' I continued , 'in future, at rehearsals you will bear in mind the exhortations of Noel Coward, that is, remember your lines and don't bump into the furniture. Apart from that, don't interfere. Got it?'

He stared at me for a moment or two, but I held his gaze until he looked away, then nodded. 'OK, fine,' he said.

'Good lad!' I exclaimed cheerfully and clapped him on the shoulder, 'I knew we would see eye to eye!'

'And you won't say anything to my wife?' he asked.

'Say anything about what?' I said with bright-eyed innocence and took my leave.

I found the party – Marcus, Janet, Tom and to my surprise, Derek – sitting in our usual corner at Et Alia and pulled up a stool. A new bottle of wine was ordered and Marcus filled the glasses.

Derek cleared his throat, 'I won't interrupt you for long, but I was just passing when I bumped into Janet here and she insisted on me joining you for a drink.'

'Nice to see you again, Derek,' I said. 'It's been too long!'

He looked at me with a quizzical air. 'I don't know about that, young Ben,' he said, 'but anyway, I wanted you to know that I have been persuaded to come back to CAOS and resume the role of the Duke.'

'Ah,' I replied, 'and that was because you heard what a hash I was making of it, I suppose?'

Derek raised his hand as if pushing away an unwelcome thought. 'No, no, of course not. Not at all,' he said, then added. 'Well, not entirely,' which slightly spoiled the effect as far as I was concerned. He went on, 'No, it was really Bill Wainwright who convinced me to come back.'

'Bill Wainwright?' the rest of us chorused in puzzlement.

'Yes, Bill said it was bad for business me standing in The Wonk and complaining. And if I didn't get back to CAOS forthwith, I would be barred. That concentrated my mind wonderfully!'

We raised our glasses in salutation and I forbore to say that it had been at my request that Bill had issued such an ultimatum.

'So the only fly in the ointment is that twerp Barrett,' Derek went on.

Janet looked suddenly pale and I interrupted.

'Oh, I think you'll have no more trouble from that quarter, Derek.'

He raised an eyebrow and looked as though he was going to start asking awkward questions, but I gave a surreptitious shake of the head.

He confined himself to remarking, 'Well, I hope you're right there, Ben. Anyway, I'll be off now – must get back to The Wonk!'

With that, he drained his glass and left us.

After a short pause, Janet said, 'And now you can tell us what happened about The Manor House?'

'Yes, come on, Ben,' agreed Marcus. 'After all, we helped you out with that one.'

'Yes, OK, OK,' I held my hands up, 'give me a chance. I didn't want to say anything in front of Derek. Where should I start?'

'Well, who, what, how and why,' Marcus said impatiently, 'that's a good start!'

'Well, the who – it was Bill's cousin, Suzanne,' I replied, 'as to the what, well, we don't know exactly how much, but a fair bit over the last two years. The main fraud was of course the rooms – she was taking the money for the rooms directly, and not recording them as occupied in the hotel register.'

'But how did she manage that?' It was Tom this time.

'Well, she could only do it when she was working on reception, of course,' I started, 'which is partly how we identified that it was her, by cross referencing periods when room receipts were down compared with who was on duty at the time.'

'How did she get the punters to do it?' asked Marcus. 'Surely they would realise something was odd?'

'Oh, not necessarily,' I replied airily. 'She would offer people a hefty discount on the normal room rates if they paid in full in advance, and also say that they couldn't put drinks or meals on their room bill – they would have to pay for those at the time.'

'Yes, but what about the payments? How did she get the money to her own account?' Janet looked puzzled.

'Well, that was quite neat. She simply used her own credit card machine, which incorporated bank details of an account she had set up, and hey presto!'

Marcus said, 'But how come no one noticed these room were occupied when they should have been empty?'

I gave a rueful smile. 'Well, oddly, that was how I stumbled on her in the first place. The one thing that would have given the game away would be rooms that weren't clean for the subsequent occupants, and so, she simply cleaned them herself. When I was prowling around that evening and came across her cleaning rooms, I thought it was a bit odd. But of course, her brief was to come and go and help out with any function as necessary, so nobody else really thought anything of it.' I took a gulp of wine and added, 'And the other clever thing she did was to manipulate the occupancy rate reports, so that it looked as though they were normal.'

'And what about the bar takings?' Janet asked.

'Well, there she was, simply being a bit greedy and it was easy to see that the money was down on the occasions that she was in charge.'

Janet looked thoughtful. 'But why did she do it? I mean, obviously she wanted the money, but she must have had a fair bit anyway to be a part-owner of the place?'

I nodded. 'Yes, that's true and I was puzzled by that myself. But it came out this afternoon that when her and Bill's aunt died – which was where the money originally came from – Suzanne felt that she hadn't got her fair share.'

'So she thought she'd help herself to a bit more?' Marcus asked ironically.

I shrugged. 'I suppose so.'

Janet asked anxiously, 'You said Randall's name wasn't on the hotel register. Was he involved in any way?'

I hesitated for a second before saying, 'I don't believe so. I think Suzanne offered him a big discount if he paid in advance and he simply took advantage of her offer.' I forbore to add that I had a fair idea that Randall had taken advantage of other offers the fair Suzanne had put his way.

That, of course, was how he had been so well informed about Derek Hall – Bill must have discussed it with his cousin, Suzanne, who had in turn passed it on to Randall.

'And what will happen now?' Janet gave me one of her gimlet like looks.

I spread my hands. 'Well, that is really up to Bill and the other members of the syndicate. Obviously there are certain things I have to report for professional reasons, but it is up to them as to whether they bring the police into it. I suspect that they will keep it quiet for the sake of the business and sort it out between them.'

'So all's well that ends well!' Tom said brightly, raising a glass in salutation.

Marcus joined in, adding, 'Yes, you've sorted out The Manor House, you've got Derek to come back and you've apparently sorted Randall out too! Not a bad day's work, I would say!' He paused, then added, 'Though I suppose it means you're back to being just Francesco.'

'Well, if it's for the greater good of the society…' I started to say in my most pompous tone, but the others started laughing. So I desisted and instead tried to look suitably modest as they clinked glasses.

Even Janet joined in, though, a cloud suddenly came across her face, and she said, 'Just a second, before you get carried away. Isn't there a staff appraisal you haven't done yet?'

'Is there?' I asked innocently.

Janet gave a contemptuous snort. 'Of course there is. What about mine?'

'Ah yes,' I went, and reached in a pocket. 'In fact, I have it here. Should I read it to you? It's very short.'

After a slight hesitation, Janet nodded.

'In fact, it consists of only five letters. PPIEW.'

Janet looked puzzled. 'PPIEW?'

'Yes,' I replied triumphantly, 'which of course stands for "practically perfect in every way".'

The others laughed as Janet said, 'Hmph! And quite right too!'

5. Ben Jonson and the Spirit of Christmas

There are certain events in office life which I find oddly depressing. One of these is our financial year end. This may surprise my colleagues, family and friends, because, if I may say so without undue hubris, Jonson & Co Forensic Accountants has actually performed rather well over the years, and I see a steady increase in all the fundamentals of turnover, profit and, most importantly, cash. The latter is of course vital, and I have the saying, "Turnover is vanity, profit is reality, but cash is king," hanging opposite my desk, where my eye falls on it every day.

But as I was saying, the year end, even if we have done well, causes me some vague feelings of depression, since, I think to myself, we have to start all over again for the new financial year and who knows what that will bring?

One other annual trial is Christmas. No, not Christmas itself, which I actually love, although it is true that it is not the same since my wife, Julia, died. It is the Christmas season in the office which I find trying, culminating, of course, in the office Christmas Party.

I can tell it is December the first without consulting the calendar, because as I enter the office an artificial Christmas tree has mysteriously been placed in the reception area, whilst Christmas music plays relentlessly over the audio system. I remember saying to my old pal Tom Bremner one night in one of our convivial meetings in the wine bar just down the high street, 'If I hear "Rockin' around the friggin' Christmas tree" one more time, I swear I will rip out the loudspeakers with my bare hands.'

One morning, as I was composing a carefully crafted letter to the water supplying company for the area, pointing out that if their meter readings were anything like correct, the office would by now have floated away down the high street like Noah's Ark, Janet, my imperious office manager, swept into my room and stood over me.

'Christmas!' she exclaimed.

I looked up from my desk. 'Twenty-fifth of December, normally,' I replied sarcastically. 'Anything else you need to know?'

Janet rolled her eyes heavenward. Then with exaggerated patience she said, 'The office Christmas party, I mean.' She tapped her foot impatiently. 'Plus other Christmas arrangements, of course,' she added.

I leant back in my chair. The other "arrangements" she referred to were twofold. One was simply the days on which the office would be closed over the Christmas period. This was fairly easy to establish and I had long ago given up any hope of trying to keep the place open between Boxing Day and New Year, so the staff had the time off, with the stipulation it came out of their annual entitlement.

In a fit of generosity one year, I had declared that Christmas Eve would also be a holiday, but this was in addition to the normal leave. It was done on the basis that no chargeable time was done on this day, as the staff were too busy giving each other Christmas gifts and munching liqueur chocolates to do anything useful. They also tended to slope off to the pub around 12 o'clock – either to The Wonk for the beer drinkers, or to my preferred establishment, Et Alia, for the rest.

I sighed inwardly. All that chargeable time lost! Then in addition, the cash flow was severely disrupted since every other business was in the same position. So the payments of invoices tended to dry up around the middle of the month and normal service, so to speak, did not resume until well into the middle of January. I had on occasion voiced these concerns, but had been accused of being like Ebenezer Scrooge, who, I had come to consider, was a much misunderstood figure...

Then the other matter was the annual Christmas bonus. Now I have been trying for years to do away with this incubus, on the grounds that it satisfies no one. As an employer, I naturally resent paying it and the staff too never seem satisfied. If you do it on a pure percentage basis, then of course the people on lower salaries do not think they have got very much. If you do it on a flat basis, that is, the same amount for everyone, then the higher earners start to complain. If you start introducing factors such as the length of service, then that causes problems when you find the office junior, who has been with us for several years, gets rather more than the recently appointed senior manager. If you start adding further layers of criteria, then the whole process gets ridiculously complicated and time consuming.

So this year, I took the bull by the horns, so to speak, and declared that from now on the annual salary review would incorporate the bonus. And that of course caused a whole further round of dissatisfaction. It took considerable effort and patience, not to mention money, of course, on my part to bring the staff around to my way of thinking. I thought I had succeeded, but Janet soon disabused me of *that* comforting thought.

'Since you have seen fit to abolish the Christmas bonus,' she began, and although I opened my mouth to protest that I had not *abolished* it, but rather realigned it, Janet swept on regardless, 'then perhaps you could make a bit more effort as regards the Christmas party this year.'

'Well, I don't know what was wrong with last year…' I began, but Janet cut me off.

'What was wrong with it?' she snapped. 'There was very little right with it. I told you that having it here in the office was a big mistake.'

'I was trying to keep the costs down,' I protested, but Janet cut me off again.

'Keep the costs down? It cost a fortune to repair the photocopier for one thing. And the stationery cupboard door has never been the same either.'

'What, ever since that business with old Creepy Crawley?' I tried to suppress a grin but I think I failed utterly, as Janet went off again.

'It's no laughing matter! He could have been seriously hurt. And as for Alison, well, it took her weeks to get over it.'

I nodded gravely and pretended to look sympathetically concerned. It had all been due to Alex "Creepy" Crawley's unfortunate squint, which, exacerbated by a few too many glasses of Christmas cheer, had led Alison, otherwise known as Alice in Ledgerland, to assume he was giving her a "come hither" invitation into the privacy of the stationery cupboard.

Alison, who is, let us say, of comfortable proportions, had launched herself at the hapless Creepy and he, in a last-ditch effort to avoid her, had tripped heavily over a decorative planter and ended up on the floor. Alison, meanwhile, had collided with the door, causing it to come off its hinges. It had all been rather unfortunate and had caused a certain embarrassment for all concerned on the next days in the office. And of course, as Janet had intimated, the photocopier had borne the brunt of numerous inebriated partygoers trying to make facsimiles of their nether regions...

But I was forced to agree with Janet: the office is not the place for parties. Apart from anything else, finding for weeks afterward discarded portions of egg sandwiches and pizza slices in every nook and cranny was less than appealing.

And then there was the thorny problem of whether to invite partners or not. For some years, I had decided to restrict the function purely to employees of the firm, but repeated pleas to include husbands, wives, fiancés and other hangers on had caused me to relent. That was the year we had tried taking a few tables at a local hotel for their Christmas so-called ball. The meal had been frightful: Brussels sprouts the size of cabbages and the consistency of mild steel, combined with roast turkey consisting of well-developed drumsticks presumably from the legs on which the poor creatures habitually roosted. Then the bar bill had been astronomic, as the hangers-on had taken full advantage of the "free-bar" policy before the meal and had downed quite remarkable quantities of "shots" and other exotic drinks, including, as I recall, a dubious concoction consisting of Tia Maria and blackcurrant juice. By the time the disco started, most of our party were barely capable of standing, let alone performing the birdy song or locomotion. And so the following year we had reverted to a strict "employees-only" regime.

However, lately, there had been murmurings that this policy should be reversed yet again and the party should also involve some dance music.

'OK, OK, Janet,' I knew when it was best to retreat gracefully, 'let's look at some possible places for Christmas, should we? But can we leave it for now…' I didn't get any further, as the phone on my desk trilled. And before I could reach it, Janet had snatched up the receiver.

'Jonson and Co,' she barked, in a manner reminiscent of a Kalashnikov, then listened for a moment before passing the receiver to me and mouthing "Tom Bremner" at me.

Tom, of course, is my old chum and drinking companion, who also happens to be senior partner at a firm of solicitors just down the high street from my office, and a regular and profitable source of work for my firm.

'That you, Ben?' Tom's *basso profundo* boomed out from the handset. And after I confirmed indeed that was the case, he went on, 'Got a nice little one for you here, old boy. Accident claim.'

I expressed thanks, though, to be honest, I was slightly disappointed, as accident cases very often are rather run-of-the-mill affairs. And although they can undoubtedly be profitable as far as I was concerned, the process of preparing a report can be unexciting. I thanked him again for his instructions and he rang off with a promise to send the papers over to me shortly and an invitation to join him at close of play, so to speak, at our favourite haunt, Et Alia, the wine bar on the high street located conveniently between our two offices.

I was relieved to find that Janet had gone about her business by the time I had replaced the telephone on its holder, and I settled down to work. It was only about half an hour later that I was interrupted again by Janet, this time bearing a package which I surmised was from Tom.

'This is for you,' she said shortly, banging the parcel down on my desk with such force that all my pens rolled off onto the floor. As I was groping around my chair trying to retrieve them, she continued, 'And another thing: what are we going to do for the CAOS Christmas show? Clive has us down for a duet.'

But I felt that we had discussed Christmas activities enough for one day and I said firmly, 'It's only April, for goodness's sake! Let's talk about that another time please, Janet. I want to look at this package now.'

With some reluctance, Janet left me once more, and I turned my attentions to the parcel. As I had guessed, it was indeed from Tom and contained the files relating to a personal injury claim against our local council.

I sighed. 'Another boring routine accident case! Oh well, at least it's easy money.'

But little did I know, I could not have been more wrong...

As it happened, other matters intervened, and I had not had the opportunity for anything more than a cursory glance at the file before I left the office that evening. I hurried down the high street, entered the wine bar Et Alia and espied in our usual corner my old pal Tom and to my surprise, next to him, Marcus. Although I had messaged Marcus to tell him where I was going, he had not responded.

The two of them were in earnest conversation and did not look up until I plonked myself down at the table and asked, 'Anything left in that bottle?'

They both jumped and Tom with a broad grin poured some wine into a glass which he had thoughtfully already obtained.

'What were you two so deep in conversation about?' I asked as lightly as I could.

The truth is, I get a little nervous when Marcus and Tom are huddled together, because it generally means that they are colluding on some parody of a G&S song, usually at my expense.

'Oh, Marcus here was just picking my brains, such as they are, about work. He needs to come up with some names for a new drug.'

Marcus works in marketing and is actually quite high-powered. He had asked me the same thing the previous evening, although I had to admit to being rather stumped. 'And have you thought of anything?' I asked.

Marcus replied before Tom could speak. 'Actually, he's been very helpful. More use than you anyway.' He cuffed me playfully on the head, almost causing me to spill my drink. I spluttered in protest, but he carried on. 'Yes, Tom's come up with "Chlolixsin" and "Akanixtyl" not to mention "Athelas".'

'They all sound very convincing,' I affirmed, 'though the last one does sound vaguely familiar. What's the drug for?'

'Well, I just wanted some general ideas really,' said Marcus, 'but there is a new mouthwash that we haven't got a final name for yet, which was what Tom was focussing on.'

I was still mulling over "Athelas" and whipped out my phone to check the name.

'Aha!' I cried triumphantly, 'I thought it sounded familiar. It's a name dreamed up by Tolkien in *The Lord of the Rings*. Apparently it's a sweet-smelling herb with healing powers and is used for curing wounds and counteracting evil influences like the "Black Breath".' I finished reading my screen.

Tom and Marcus looked crestfallen. 'Well, that's no good then!' exclaimed Marcus.

'Oh, I don't know – useful if you're under attack from the Black Riders, perhaps,' I replied dryly.

As Marcus went off rather disconsolately to the bar to fetch another bottle of wine, Tom turned to me and asked, 'Did you have a chance to look at that file I sent you?'

'I had a quick glance, yes,' I replied, 'but perhaps you could just give me a quick resume?'

'Yes, sure,' Tom said, 'well, let's see now. The claimant in question is one Ryan Simmons, aged 34, and he is claiming

144

damages from the Council after an accident in the park, about four months ago.'

'Yes, I got that bit,' I said, 'what happened to him?'

Tom drained his glass and sat contemplating the dregs for a moment. 'Ryan had been out for the evening with his best mate, Scott Edwards, and they were making their way to the taxi rank by the station so took a short cut through the park. Whilst they were walking through it, Ryan tripped over a pothole on the path, injuring himself sufficiently badly that Scott felt obliged to call for an ambulance. It turned out that Ryan had actually broken his leg. As he is a self-employed builder, this was obviously pretty serious as regards working and so he is suing the council for damages. That's it in a nutshell. And your job, of course, is to come up with a suitable figure!'

'Right, well that's clear enough, I think. I'll get someone on it first thing in the morning.'

Just then, Marcus arrived with a fresh bottle. 'Any more ideas?' he asked

I thought for a second. 'Fidrocin?' I hazarded.

Marcus considered this. 'Mmm, yes, well, it has the right sort of ring, I suppose, but it doesn't really tell you what the product will do, does it?'

'Anyway' I hurried on, 'more importantly, I'm looking for a venue for our office Christmas festivities. I've got Janet chasing me about it so I need to come up with something. What are you doing, Tom?'

'We're having a dinner dance at The Metropole,' Tom replied, rather grandly. The Metropole was a very swanky five-star hotel in the neighbouring town and was renowned for being outrageously expensive.

'Including partners?' I queried in a vain hope that Tom would say no.

'Of course including partners,' he replied rather impatiently.

Marcus piped up, 'We're thinking of New York this year!'

'Including partners?' I asked, hopefully.

Marcus just gave me a withering look, which I took to be a "no".

'Well, I don't think either of those is suitable for my outfit,' I said firmly, 'but I don't want it in the office again, not after last time.'

In response to the looks of query, I outlined the events of last year. After the laughter had died down, I said, 'Anyway, I need to come up with something. Any thoughts?'

Tom said, 'I have heard that The Black Horse is not bad these days.'

'What? The Wonk?' I asked incredulously. 'It's an absolute dive.'

'Oh, it's been tarted up since you were last there,' said Tom airily. 'Looks quite different.'

'Well, it's been quite some while since that affair at The Manor House, which was the last time I patronised The Wonk,' I mused, 'I suppose it's worth a look...'

As I had promised Tom, the next morning I looked at my team's work schedules to find someone to work on the case of Ryan Simmons. As luck would have it, we were pretty busy, so I rang through to Alex "Creepy" Crawley and asked him to step through. He duly appeared in my office a few minutes later, creeping silently up to my desk unobserved by me as I pored over some files and making me jump when he said softly, 'You wanted to see me, Ben?'

'What? Oh yes, I did, Alex,' I replied, trying to resist the temptation to slide sideways in my chair to get into his apparent line of fire.

I quickly outlined the case and ended by adding, 'Don't forget this guy is self-employed,' I said to him. 'This needs a little bit more thought than just looking at a few payslips!'

This was met with what could be described as a disdainful look, although since the look was directed at a low sofa to the left of my desk, it was slightly difficult to be sure.

I had hardly settled back to work again when Janet appeared before me clutching what looked to be sheets of music. 'We must talk about the CAOS Christmas concert,' she started.

'Must we?' I answered.

Janet pierced me with one of her gimlet looks. 'Yes, we must. We need all the practice we can get.'

'But we've got months to go yet,' I protested.

'Maybe, but we've got another show to do between now and then, haven't we, so we need to be prepared.'

I groaned inwardly. Janet went on, 'Anyway, I thought that 1920s' song *You're the Cream in My Coffee* would be nice. We could dress up in period costume.'

I winced as I had a mental picture of Janet in a flapper outfit wafting a feather boa about the stage. 'Yes, well possibly—' I started but Janet was in full flow.

'I was practising it over the weekend with my sister, Trudi …'

An image came to me of Janet's sibling, whom I had briefly met some while ago. A pale face with staring eyes and pouting lips. 'Oh, and how is the old trout…er…I mean dear Trudi?' I enquired politely.

Janet ignored the interruption and pressed on regardless. 'And we worked on some choreography…' She stopped, having presumably noted my less than enthusiastic response. 'Well, have you got a better idea?' she snapped.

'Actually, I was thinking more of a novelty type number,' I replied evenly.

'Oh yes,' Janet enthused, 'not a bad idea. How about "Itsy-bitsy, teeny-weeny, yellow polka-dot bikini?".'

I shuddered. If the idea of Janet in a short skirt was less than appealing, then the prospect of her in *that* outfit was positively terrifying. My eye alighted on the calendar on the wall, which featured rather lurid photographs of "Great Cities of the World".

'I had a couple of ideas,' I said mendaciously, 'for instance, *A Windmill in Old Amsterdam*?'

The lips went as thin as dental floss, so I hurried on, 'Or *Wonderful, Wonderful Copenhagen*. That could work.' The lips went thinner still. 'Or *Istanbul not Constantinople*?

Something about Paris? Or New York,' I tried again, with one eye still on the wall opposite. 'There's a range of options there from the funny to the romantic.'

The look on Janet's face was hardly encouraging. A thought struck me and I tried a different tack. 'Or really,' I mused, 'as it is an operatic society, and we do mainly G&S, how about something from one of their operettas?'

Janet considered this for a moment then nodded and said, 'Well, that's reasonable, I suppose. Although Clive didn't stipulate it had to be G&S. Did you have anything in mind?'

Actually, I had. As I may have mentioned before, I have always rather had a fancy to perform the role of The Lord Chancellor in *Iolanthe*. In fact, that was the main reason I had joined the local amateur operatic society, although I had to admit that judging by my performances to date, it was a little unlikely that I would ever be cast in that part. However, nothing ventured, nothing gained, so I said casually, 'Oh, I don't know, how about the *Nightmare Song* from *Iolanthe*?'

Janet's lips compressed yet further. 'Wonderful idea,' she said in a brittle tone. 'Just one slight snag.'

'And what's that?'

'It's not a duet! What would I be doing whilst you're performing?' she snapped.

It was a fair point but I put in briskly, 'Oh, couldn't you waft about around me in a fairy costume or something?'

I was treated to a full-bore, double barrel look of contempt.

'I don't see myself as wafting anywhere, thank you very much,' she replied coldly. 'Perhaps we'd better think again.'

'Yes, well, perhaps you're right,' I said and in an endeavour to change the subject, I added, 'And that reminds me, I've been looking in to the office party.'

'Oh yes?' said Janet. 'Any conclusion?'

'No, not yet,' I replied. 'But someone did suggest The Wonk, so I thought I'd go up there tonight with Marcus and see what it's like.'

I had not in fact mentioned this to Marcus at all, but I wanted to give the appearance of being on the case, as it were.

To judge from the expression on Janet's face, I could see that she was less than impressed with the idea of The Wonk, so I added in a defensive tone, 'It's been tarted up recently, and it's supposed to be much better now. Anyway, I'll let you know.'

'Make sure you do,' was the short reply and to my relief, Janet left the room.

By a stroke of luck, I was out of the office at various meetings for the rest of the day and most of the next, which was just as well, as needless to say, we had not ventured as far as The Wonk in the evening. I called in at my office late the next afternoon to find that for once Janet had left early. I noticed on my desk a report from Alex "Creepy" Crawley, labelled "Ryan Simmons", picked it up and put it into my case with the intention of reading it at home later.

Around six, I locked up and made my way down the high street to my home. As I turned in the gateway, I noticed with some dismay an old Nissan in the drive. This belonged to my cleaner, Freda Bell, known to us colloquially as "Freda-wot-does". Freda is a bustling woman in her late fifties, who has been "doing" for my family for years, having been recruited by my late wife, Julia, whilst the children were still quite small.

Now I am the first to agree that Freda is an excellent cleaner and she seems to know instinctively what needs to be done in the house without my having to say anything. She is intensely loyal and was devoted to Julia, and now, perhaps more surprisingly, has become devoted to Marcus. She refers to us as "Mr J" and "Mr Marcus" – she would never be so informal as to call us by our first names alone.

She does however have her foibles. The main one is a tendency to lard her conversation with Malapropisms and mangled metaphors to the extent that it is hard to fathom what she is talking about. Combine this with a penchant for long rambling stories about people I have never heard of and I try, if I can, to avoid any face-to-face contact. This is in contrast to Marcus, who seems to positively revel in her company. So it was not altogether surprising to find the two of them sitting at the breakfast bar, nursing large mugs of tea.

Freda was in full flow. 'And so I says, "You can plead with me until the cows come home blue in the face!"'

Marcus was all agog at this thrilling tale. 'Go on,' he urged.

Freda complied with alacrity. 'And then I says to her, "Let me just play Devil's avocado for a moment..." Oh, hello, Mr J, didn't see you there. Like a nice cuppa?'

I declined the offer of tea, but added, 'Don't let me interrupt your story, Freda, please,' with what I thought was a fairly hefty dose of irony.

This was, of course, totally wasted on her, but it had the desired effect of making her get down from the stool and say, 'Oh, no, better be on my way. I'm late as it is and Mr Bell will be giving me the Spanish Armada when I get home!'

She exited the room whilst I rolled my eyes heavenwards.

Marcus grinned broadly. 'Drink?' he offered.

I shook my head. 'No thanks. I thought we'd wander up to The Wonk in a while and give it the once-over. I'll have a drink then.'

Marcus shrugged. 'I think it's a waste of time if you're thinking about your office bash, but OK. When do you want to go?'

'Just give me half an hour or so, will you? There's a report I want to read before we set off.'

Freda, now wearing a mac and scarf, stuck her head round the door and announced, 'I'll be off now. I'll tell you the rest of that story next time, Mr Marcus. You'll have to wait until then – it's a real cliff-dweller, isn't it?'

I retreated to the study with my case, sat at my desk and took out the file, then settled back to read.

I lost myself in the report for the next thirty minutes.

I had to admit, old Creepy Crawley may have his own quirks, but he was pretty astute. Although Ryan's reported profit for the previous two years had been modest, Alex had, after a long discussion with him, found out that in this time,

Ryan had renovated a run-down property he had purchased and converted some outbuildings into two holiday lets.

Taking account of the value of this time, looked at in a variety of ways, meant that the theoretical profit was actually quite considerable. There was an interim calculation from the Council, which had merely used the accounts figures, so that, using Alex's calculations, the claim would be at least three times that amount.

Marcus stuck his head round the door and asked, 'Ready for the off?'

I thrust the file back in my case and jumped up. 'Certainly! Let's rock and roll!'

We left the house and set off up the high street. Marcus suddenly said, 'I know we're doing this for your office party, but what about *our* Christmas this year?'

My heart sank a little. Much as I like Christmas, there is an awkwardness these days. This revolves around my children, Sam and Amy. Whilst I love having them to stay at Christmas, there are a few problems. One, of course, is that they now have boyfriends and girlfriends of their own, and there is the dilemma of where they should go over the festive season. Then there is the issue of Marcus. Whilst the kids in general terms have been remarkably accepting of me and Marcus, this only really applies when they are away from home. As soon as they come back, and Marcus is around, there is a distinct frisson in the atmosphere. Amy is better at covering it up and always makes a point of engaging with him.

Sam, however, is much more edgy and tends to keep aloof. For his part, I know Marcus tries his best, but sometimes he almost tries too hard. Although usually Marcus is not the least bit camp, somehow in his eagerness to please, he lurches into it. For instance, by enthusing over a new outfit Amy is wearing and being a little too *florid,* shall we say, in his mannerisms. Then I can see the look on Sam's face and I in turn get flustered and try too hard to be normal, so to speak. I feel torn in different directions at the same time.

I love all these people, I think to myself, *and I think they love me, so why can't we all just get on together?*

I tried to sound insouciant. 'Oh, the normal, I think. Of course, I haven't actually brought the subject up with the kids – it's far too early for them to have thought about it. But I will do, soon.'

Marcus nodded, 'Yes, I suppose so. I just thought…' his voice trailed off.

'Thought what?' I asked, but Marcus just shrugged and said,

'Oh, doesn't matter. Look here we are. After you,' and he held the door for me, giving a slight bow in mock obeisance as I entered.

I looked round at the bar. It did not seem so very different from the last time I had been there. The gaming machines were still in the far corner and it even looked like the same two youths were playing on them. True, there was a slight smell of new paint and the colour on the walls was perhaps a moderately less dingy shade of beige, but as to fundamentals, there appeared no very great alteration.

'I think we're wasting our time,' I muttered, *sotto voce,* to Marcus, but he propelled me forward towards the lounge bar, saying, 'Well, you might as well ask, now we're here. And I could do with a drink!'

We walked up to the bar, where I could see that the landlord, Bill Wainwright, was serving another customer. Although I could only see the back of him, I recognised the figure straightaway.

'Hello, Randall. Didn't expect to see you in here.'

Randall Barrett turned and ran his eye up and down me, as though inspecting some particularly repellent arachnid, but he answered civilly enough, 'Evening, Ben. I could say the same to you.'

I was about to explain, but Marcus interrupted by saying eagerly, 'Hello, Randall. How are you?'

Now Marcus has a bit of a "thing" about Randall and goes visibly weak at the knees when they meet. I think Randall is perfectly well aware of this, and although his interests, so to speak, lie elsewhere, he never fails to play up to Marcus.

In part, I think he does it to annoy me, but it could also be that his ego is such that he responds in this way to any attention, male or female. I was therefore irritated, but not surprised, when Randall clasped Marcus's hand with his trademark two-handed shake and followed this up by putting an arm around Marcus's shoulder and giving him a squeeze, whilst simultaneously breathing in a stage whisper into his ear, 'All the better for seeing you!'

Marcus, for want of a better phrase, came over "all unnecessary" by flushing a deep red, and immediately started running his finger around the "V" in his shirt.

'Better make yours a large one,' I said, somewhat waspishly, to Marcus as I turned to Bill and ordered our drinks. 'And could I have a word with you please, Bill, about your Christmas functions? I'm looking for somewhere for our office party,' I added.

'Certainly, Ben. I'll be with you in a few minutes,' Bill replied.

By this time, Randall had sloped off to a dark corner where I could see him at a table with a young woman sporting long, blonde hair.

'And that lady is certainly not Mrs Barrett,' I nudged Marcus and nodded in Randall's direction. 'Looks like he's up to his old tricks again.'

'Yes, he is a bit of a lad, isn't he?' Marcus replied in almost a tone of admiration, irritating me further.

I was about to proselytise on the virtue of fidelity in a relationship, but at that moment Bill reappeared and asked, 'Now, how can I help you two gents?'

I explained what I wanted, and Bill handed over some price lists, adding, 'Of course, the disco is included in that. And the karaoke.'

My heart sank but I bravely asked if we could see the function room. Bill led us back through the saloon and into a vast room at the back of the pub. Again, there was a faint smell of new paint, but otherwise the room looked unchanged from the nineteen-seventies. Obviously noting my less than rapturous expression, Bill added, 'Of course it looks quite different when it's all decorated for Christmas and full of people. Quite an atmosphere.'

'Quite an atmosphere – just like a clinic!' Marcus whispered as we followed Bill back to the lounge bar.

I cleared my throat and said to Bill, 'Great, thanks for that, Bill. I'll have a think and let you know.'

We finished our drinks and prepared to leave. Randall arrived back at the bar at that moment and seeing him again reminded me of something.

'Funny, I was just reading one of your medical reports this afternoon,' I said to him brightly. 'Accident claim I'm working on. Chap who tripped over a pothole just down the road here and broke his leg.'

Randall's eyes narrowed. 'Mmm. Well, I do reports all the time and obviously I couldn't discuss them with you here…'

'No, no, of course not—' I interrupted hurriedly, 'I wouldn't dream of asking that. Just it was a bit of a coincidence seeing you, that's all.'

Randall carried on without pausing, 'But I do know the one you mean. Pothole, you say?'

I was about to reply when his companion appeared and Randall, clearly not wishing to introduce us, grabbed her by the elbow and ushered her back to her seat, with a quick shout of 'Same again, Bill, please' as he went.

Marcus and I took our leave, though I couldn't resist a cheery wave to Randall and his companion as we went, which he studiously ignored.

We stepped out into High Street. 'I don't know why you always have to make such a fool of yourself when you meet Randall,' I began, somewhat recklessly, intending some harmless leg-pulling at Marcus's expense.

Marcus turned and hissed at me, 'I don't know what you're talking about! Don't be ridiculous!'

And with that, he spun away and stormed up the road, his leather-soled shoes clapping angrily on the damp pavement like the keys of a typewriter.

I was taken aback. I shouted after him, 'Marcus! Hey, Marcus! Wait!' but he didn't pause.

Dammit! I thought to myself and stared after him.

'Better cut along home and try to patch things up,' I muttered and set off in pursuit.

Marcus is somewhat taller than I am with a considerably longer stride, so that I found myself breaking into a trot to try to catch up. I finally got near him and grabbed his arm.

'Marcus, please, I'm sorry!' I said, and he slowed then stopped. I went on, 'Look, Marcus, I didn't mean anything. I was just going to wind you up a bit, that's all.'

Marcus turned toward me and in the sickly yellow of the street-light, I could see he had tears in his eyes. He said, 'Yes, I know really. I'm sorry too. I don't know what came over me.'

I had a funny feeling I knew, but decided it would be better to refrain from saying it. 'Come on, old lad,' I said, 'let's get home and have a decent glass of wine.'

He nodded and fell into step alongside me and we carried on up the road. I talked as we went, trying both to soothe Marcus and bolster him up, but at the back of my mind, something was nagging away at me, though I couldn't quite pin down what it was…

Over a drink and a plate of shepherd's pie, which he had fortunately prepared earlier, Marcus recovered his sangfroid once more and we ended the evening happily discussing possible duets for me to perform with Janet at the CAOS Christmas concert.

'How about that thing *Baby, It's Cold Outside*?' suggested Marcus. 'It should be sort of seasonal for a start. And I remember seeing it done with a sort of role reversal, so that the chap does the girl's part in a very clipped, British upper-class accent. It was very funny.'

I considered this. 'Yes, I know the one. Actually, that's not a bad idea. It could work very well. I'll print the lyrics off and suggest it to her tomorrow.'

I was as good as my word and for once caught Janet unawares as I bounced into her room the next morning and, with a flourish, presented her with the lyrics to the song.

'For the Christmas concert,' I said. 'Let me know what you think,' and I waltzed away before she could reply.

I had a couple of back-to-back meetings out of the office and it was mid-afternoon before I returned. As I sat in my desk chair, unpacking files from my case, I became aware of a presence and looked up to find Janet glowering at me. She was holding what looked suspiciously like the lyrics that I had handed to her that morning and judging by her expression, not only was it cold outside, it was decidedly icy inside as well.

'Can I help you, Janet?' I asked coolly, matching my tone of voice to the atmosphere.

'This!' she cried, brandishing the sheet of lyrics. 'It won't do!'

'Won't do?' I expressed astonishment. 'Why ever not?'

'Well, I had a discussion with my feminist group at lunchtime and we all felt that the words are aggressive and inappropriate.'

'Aggressive and inappropriate? What do you mean?' I retorted.

Janet sighed and crossed her arms. 'It's all about a man trying to dissuade a woman from leaving a party despite her repeated protestations that she has to go home. Totally inappropriate in this day and age. So we've made some alterations.' She thrust some sheets of paper into my hand.

I glanced down the page and began to splutter. 'You can't be serious!' I began. 'This is ridiculous!'

'Why?' Janet shot back.

I took some deep breaths and tried to stay calm. 'Well, see here. The original line in the song is "My mother will start to worry / Beautiful, what's your hurry?" and you've replaced it with: "My mother will start to worry/ Call her to tell her you're fine!"'

'Seems a perfectly reasonable response in the circumstances,' Janet retorted.

I tried again. 'And how about here. The line is: "Say, what's in this drink?/ No cabs to be had out there" and you've changed it to: "Say what's in this drink?/ It's non-alcoholic peach juice, actually."'

Janet folded her arms. 'The original line was very dubious. It sounds as if he might be slipping Rohypnol in her martini or something. Appalling. The important thing is to emphasise consent.'

I sighed. 'Well, apart from the fact that my idea was to reverse the roles, so that you would be putting something in *my* drink, I think it sounds ridiculous. And if you're determined to change the words like that, we'll just have to forget it and come up with something different.'

Janet looked as though she was about to argue, but I silenced her by pointing at the door and saying, 'Now unless you have something to discuss concerning work, please leave and let me get on!'

With a face that could have curdled milk at a hundred yards, Janet silently exited my room. Still seething inside, I returned to my labours. The phone went just then. I picked it up, noting it was my direct line, and it turned out to be Tom Bremner.

'Got your report on the Ryan Simmons case, Ben,' he boomed. 'Looks like a good sum for him – much better than the local authority are suggesting. I'll speak to Ryan then put it forward. Hopefully we can get it agreed quite quickly.'

'Yes, fine, thanks for letting me know, Tom,' I replied and after a few other pleasantries, put the phone down and returned to work.

That evening, as I walked up the path to my front door, I noted with some irritation that "Freda-wot-does's" car was in the driveway, and even more annoyingly, I then discovered that Marcus wasn't home yet, so that I was treated to Freda's attention at full bore, so to speak. She was seated at the breakfast bar in the kitchen, busily polishing silver, a job that she likes to do frequently, to the extent that the silver plate on various artefacts is wearing dangerously thin.

I was trying to think of an excuse to go out again and the first thing that came into my mind was the Ryan Simmons case, so I said, 'Hi, Freda, I'm not stopping. Got to go out again. Are you all right?'

'Oh, hello, Mr J. Yes, I'm fine, though my doctor has told me to take it steady. He says I'm suffering from insipid hypertension.'

I paused for a second, trying to work this out before light dawned. 'Ah, I think you mean *incipient* hypertension, Freda. Unless of course it's just a very weak form.' I laughed at my own witticism, but Freda just stared at me blankly. 'Anyway,' I went on, 'just remembered, I need to go and walk up to The Wonk.'

Freda paused from her polishing for a second and said, 'Oh, it's lovely in there, isn't it? Especially now it's been done up. Me and my hubby go there for a drink. For a special occasion, like.'

I hastened to assure her that I was not going there for the purposes of imbibement. 'No, I need to go that way for research,' I said, somewhat pompously. 'It's for an accident claim I'm dealing with. I want to walk from the pub to the taxi rank at the station.'

'Oh yes, we do that sometimes,' Freda replied, 'if Mr B has had a few, like.'

I could have left it there. But for some reason I felt the need to provide more detail. 'Oh yes?' I said, 'well, I want to see where the accident happened. The guy tripped over a pothole on the path in the park.'

'Fancy,' Freda said, though with a marked lack of interest now, 'yes, that's quite a nice walk in the summer.'

'Oh, it wasn't the summer,' I said quickly, 'it was late one evening in January.'

'Wouldn't catch me going through there in the dark,' Freda said firmly.

She must have caught the look of enquiry on my face, as she went on, 'No lights in the park for one thing. Also, it's further that way to the cab rank. Quicker to keep to the road. Plus, there's some funny types hang round the park at night, you know.' She nodded as if to emphasise the point. 'Yes, many the times I've seen strange men coming running through there like a bat out of water!'

I wondered whether to correct this last simile and toyed with the idea of saying, 'Don't you mean like a fish out of hell?' but thought better of it.

I bade her farewell and made my escape. I had in fact intended to go only as far as Et Alia and have a quick glass of Chardonnay with my old chum Tom, but Freda's comments had set me thinking. And instead, I headed further up the high street in the direction of The Wonk once again.

Out of the mouth of babes and sucklings, I thought, but could not remember the rest of the quotation, though it would be a bit of a stretch to think of Freda as a suckling, still less a babe.

Nearing The Wonk, I branched off down the road which led to the station at a brisk pace. After a few minutes, I reached the entrance to the park and turned in through the heavy, wrought-iron gates. The path was bordered on each side at this point by tall, dense rhododendrons and I noted as Freda had said, that there were no lights to illuminate the way.

I pressed on, passing a central paved area with a few straggly yews, pausing for a moment at the spot where the accident had occurred. The hole had been filled in shortly after and the surface of the path was now smooth and even at this point. I carried on further and eventually emerged from the far gate of the park. From there, you had to double back to reach the station, in front of which was the taxi-rank. So again, Freda had been correct in saying that this was a longer route than just keeping to the footpath alongside the road.

This was all a bit odd. I retraced my steps and entered the park once again. On one of the open gates was a discoloured sign, which stated that the gates would be closed at dusk each night, although in truth, it did not look as though the gates had been actually closed for some considerable time. I decided that I had seen enough and headed for home. But as I neared Et Alia, my feet seemed to be drawn as though by an invisible thread and I found myself entering and heading for our usual table in the corner. Not entirely to my surprise, Tom was there, busily chatting to some business acquaintances. I tapped him on the shoulder and he swung around.

'Ben!' he exclaimed, 'I wasn't sure you would be coming in here tonight. Have a drink!' He raised a hand and miraculously, one of the bar staff appeared and took my order.

'I wish I could do that, Tom,' I remarked, 'somehow, I always seem by accident to have picked up Harry Potter's cloak of invisibility when I try to get a drink in here!'

'Oh, just a knack,' he said airily, putting an arm round my shoulder. 'Here, come on, let's sit down.'

We sat down and I said, 'Sorry to interrupt your conversation, Tom, but I wanted to ask you something.'

He gave an expansive wave of his hand. 'Oh don't worry. It was just idle chatter. What did you want?'

'It's about this Ryan Simmons case,' I replied in a low voice, not wishing to be overheard, 'I wondered if you had anything more in your files that you haven't passed on to me.'

He looked interested. 'Well, there might be. We usually only give you those bits which we consider relevant, of course. Is there anything in particular you wanted?'

'Well, I don't want to say too much here, but as I understand it, there was an ambulance called, wasn't there? So there should be some report from the paramedics, shouldn't there?'

Tom nodded. 'Yes, should be. I'll take a look in the morning, and send you everything I've got. But why do you ask? Is there a problem?'

I shook my head. 'No, not really. Just something I wanted to get clear in my head, that's all. Oh, and would it be all right if I asked Simmons to come to the office? Or I could go to him, if he's still not mobile.'

Tom shrugged. 'Sure, no problem. But again, why?'

It was my turn to shrug. 'Oh, it's just my way. I like to see the people we do these reports on in person. Helps get a feel for things, you know?'

Tom looked as though he was about to press me further, but I suggested we get another drink before he could say anything and turned the conversation to other matters.

Tom was as good as his word, and during the following morning, a package arrived on my desk, containing more papers on the Ryan Simmons case. I was tied up with other matters, so it was mid-afternoon before I had time to go through them. As I had surmised, there was indeed a report on the emergency call, put through by Ryan's chum, Scott Edwards. It was brief, but stated the call had been received at 23:13 pm and a transcript of the conversation recorded Scott as saying that his friend had fallen and hurt his leg badly and was unable to walk.

When asked where they were, Scott had replied that they were on the roadside not far from the railway station. This was curious, and obviously, the same thought had occurred to someone else, as there was a note saying that Scott had later explained that the injury had occurred in the park, but that at first, Ryan did not think it was too serious, and that they had managed to get out of the park before realising the extent of the damage, which was when Scott had summoned the emergency services.

I also noticed a couple of statements from both Scott and also from Patrick Simmons, Ryan's father, with whom he had been living at the time, following the break-up of his marriage. Scott's statement described the events of the evening and Patrick's backed this up by confirming that Scott and Ryan had told him that the injury had been caused when Ryan tripped on the pathway in the park.

Time to have a chat with Ryan, I thought and buzzed through to Janet to make the necessary arrangements.

There was still a frisson in the atmosphere between us since our discussion on the lyrics for the song for the Christmas concert. I toyed with the idea of making some conciliatory gesture, but before I could do so, she had slammed the phone down.

Just then, I noticed an email flash in. It was from my son, Sam, and caught my eye because he is not one for excessive communication. I thought it was probably because I had tried to talk to him on the phone earlier that week, but having failed, sent him an email, in which, among other topics, I raised the question of his movements for the coming Christmas.

He was as laconic as ever, but assured me all was well, and that it was a bit early for definitive plans, though he was sure he would be there. I was comforted by that, but felt uneasy by his last line: *What's Marcus doing for the festive season?*

Sam also issued an invitation to come down for a weekend soon, but I was struck by the limitations of the English language in some circumstances. In this case it was the "you" in 'Why don't you come for a weekend soon?' Was this a singular or a plural "you"? In other words, was Marcus included in the invitation? My feeling was that he was not: he has never been asked to Sam's flat before, and the little question "What's Marcus doing for the festive season?" carried with it an implication that Sam rather hoped Marcus would be elsewhere.

Not for the first time, I felt as if I was being torn in two by those closest to me. Before I could reply to Sam, however, the phone went, confirming my appointment with friend Ryan the next day. I decided to try to settle down to work and banish all thoughts of my private life from my mind for a few hours, which I did, but with only limited success.

When I returned home that evening, I was relieved to see that the old Nissan was not there. Marcus, however, was home and poured me a glass of wine as I came into the kitchen.

'Cheers, thanks, you're a pal!' I said, raising my glass to him.

'You look as though you could do with it,' he replied. 'Had a bad day?'

'No, not really,' I responded, 'though I've got a few things going around my head.'

Marcus looked quizzical, so I continued.

'One of them is Christmas. No,' I went on, putting up my hand as Marcus looked as though he was about to interrupt, 'I know it's massively early, but I need to have things fixed. You started to mutter something about it the other night, but you stopped. What were you going to say?'

Marcus didn't reply straightaway, but topped up his glass of wine from the bottle on the worktop. He waved it enquiringly at me, but I shook my head. 'I'm OK at the moment, thanks. Go on.'

Marcus took a deep breath then said in gabble, 'You know I said my company are planning our Christmas do in New York? Well, I thought perhaps you could come too and we could stay on for Christmas. I know lots of people over there – it could be good!'

He must have seen my face, because all of a sudden, he looked crestfallen. I went and put an arm around his shoulder. 'Marcus, it sounds great, but I can't. The kids, you know. I can't not see them at Christmas.'

Marcus wriggled away from me. 'No, well, I might have known,' he said stiffly, 'they always come first.'

I was ready for this. 'Yes,' I said, and I could hear the steely edge in my tone. 'Yes, they do. They will always come first. You know they have to. Please, please don't make a big thing of this. I know it's difficult sometimes, but I have my moral compass to contend with.'

Marcus merely snorted and walked out of the room. *Oh, hell!* I thought, *it's going to be a long evening!*

I went into the office in a gloomy frame of mind the next morning. Marcus had slammed out of the house a little while after our conversation, announcing that he had a squash match. He didn't return until late, after I had gone to bed, when he came into our room smelling strongly of alcohol. Perhaps unwisely, I had pretended to be asleep and he had taken himself off to another bedroom, where he was still lurking when I left for the office.

I tried to bury myself in my work but I must have looked pretty grim, as even Janet gave me a fairly wide berth. At midday, I put some papers in my case and walked back home. Janet had arranged for me to see Ryan Simmons at his father's house, where he was living and which was located a couple of miles out of town so I collected the car and set off. Simmons Senior occupied a fairly substantial Edwardian house, set back from the main road. The house itself looked newly renovated and I suspected that this had been largely down to Ryan's good offices. I rang the doorbell and a slightly coarse-looking man with a reddish complexion, who I took to be Patrick Simmons, let me in.

We introduced ourselves and Patrick led me across the hall to a small room, which was evidently used by Ryan as his office. He was on the telephone when we entered and he waved me into a seat on the opposite side of the desk at which he was sitting with his plaster-encased leg thrust out to one side. He was a good looking chap with finer features than his father and a brown rather than red complexion, surmounted by a mane of thick, chestnut brown hair, which flowed over his head in almost Pre-Raphaelite abundance.

Ryan put the phone down and reached out to shake my hand. 'Sorry, still a bit difficult to stand up,' he said with a wry smile.

'Don't worry,' I reassured him. 'How much longer will the cast be on?'

'Should be off next week, I hope,' Ryan replied. 'Can't be soon enough for me!'

'Quite,' I sympathised. 'Then I suppose it will be a few weeks of physio and so on?'

'Yes,' Ryan affirmed, nodding vigorously, 'and then I hope it won't be too long before I can get back to proper work, instead of just fiddling around behind a desk.'

He gave a snort of exasperation.

'Good, let's hope so,' I agreed. I went on, 'I'm sorry to intrude, and I know Tom Bremner has discussed this with you, but I thought it would be as well to go over a few things in our report, just to make sure we have everything complete and correct.'

I watched him narrowly whilst I said this, but Ryan replied quite casually, 'Yeah, sure, that's fine. Bring it on!'

We talked facts and figures for the next half hour, and I made a show of writing things down, although, in truth, old Creepy Crawley had made a thorough job of it. I was starting to put my file away when I asked, 'And how exactly did the accident happen again?'

Ryan said in a level tone, 'I was just walking back from The Black Horse with my friend Scott, on our way to get a taxi, when I tripped over a hole in the path. Simple as that, really.'

I nodded sympathetically. 'Dear me. It's terrible how these things happen so easily. Pity you were in the park at all – I would have thought it was quicker to use the road if you were going to the taxi rank from The Wonk...er... I mean The Black Horse.'

He shot me a look, though I pretended not to notice and I was helped by the entrance of Patrick Simmons at this point. Ryan said, 'Yes, perhaps, but Scott and I were talking so much we didn't notice where we were going.'

Vaguely possible, I thought, though the answer had come out slightly too pat to be totally convincing. 'Must have been difficult for the paramedics to retrieve you from the middle of the park?' I went on, cheerily.

Patrick answered this time. 'The pair of them didn't realise how bad Ryan was at first. Scott helped Ryan to the road and then Ryan passed out, which was when Scott dialled 999.'

I gave him a quizzical look.

He added, 'least, that's what Scott said when I saw them both up at the hospital.'

He gazed at Ryan, who nodded and said, 'Yeah, that's right.'

There was a slight pause as they both looked at me. I finished putting papers in my case and stood up. 'Oh, I see,' I said brightly, 'well, I suppose it could have been even worse. I mean, if you fall that heavily, you could have broken your wrists or arms as well, trying to save yourself. Or even a jaw or something if you'd fallen on your face.'

I held out my hand to shake Ryan's, which he did somewhat tentatively, I thought, as did Patrick. I had a feeling that my remark about other injuries had gone home. I had checked the medical record and there had been no record of any such on Ryan's arms and wrists, which was odd if the accident had happened as he had said.

I made my farewells and set off back home. I was thinking hard. I had not learnt anything conclusive from the interview, but the mood music and the exchange of looks between Ryan and his father convinced me that all was not as it seemed.

On a whim, I drove past my home and carried on up the high street, then did a right just before The Wonk following the sign for the railway station. I slowed as I approached the station and the taxi rank outside. On my right, at a higher level, was the park, separated from the road by a thick clump of trees and some iron railings. Below these there was a bank down to the road which finished with a brick wall, some three feet high, surmounted by a concrete coping.

A thought struck me and I pulled the car over to the side. Switching on the hazard-warning lights, I leapt out and crossed over. I walked along the pavement, looking at the adjoining wall, which, as the land fell away approaching the station, increased in height to around five feet. An idea was forming in my mind, but before I could get further, I noticed a traffic warden bearing down on my BMW and I hurried off to retrieve it, flashing him a sickly smile as I roared away.

I dumped the car in my drive, noting that "Freda-wot-does's" Nissan was also parked there, so hurried back to the office without entering the house.

I sat down at my desk thinking furiously. How to proceed? I thought I could do with more analysis of the medical reports on Ryan, so put a call through to Randall. I had remembered what had caused me vague disquiet the other night: it was Randall's tone when he said the word "pothole". To my surprise, he actually answered his phone, although as I was calling from the office line, he might not have recognised the number.

'Oh hi, Randall, it's Ben. Ben Jonson,' I began.

There was a silence at the other end for a few seconds, then Randall said, 'Ben. Yes. Look, if it's about last night...'

'Last night?' I was confused. 'Sorry, I don't know what you mean. No, it's about that medical report I mentioned to you the other day. Ryan Simmons, you know, the guy who broke his leg in a fall.'

'Oh, that,' Randall sounded relieved, 'what about him?'

'I wondered if you had any comments as to how the injuries were caused?'

Again there was a pause. 'That's a bit of an odd question. In the first instance, I haven't got the report in front of me, so I can't remember all the details, but in any case, I would confine myself to reporting on the injuries sustained and how they would affect his mobility and so on, and also the likely prognosis. In other words, whether there was likely to be permanent damage, for instance, or if a full recovery could be expected. The cause of the accident is not really for me to comment on.'

This was as I expected but I persisted anyway. 'OK, but did the injuries to you seem consistent with tripping over a pothole? There was no damage to the wrists and arms, was there?'

Randall said stiffly, 'I'm not sure I want to get into this conversation, Ben, or even if ethically I should do so. All I will say is that I accepted what the guy told me and that the damage was perhaps unusual, but not entirely inconsistent with a fall of the nature he described. And now I really must go, bye.'

And with that, the line went dead.

I put the receiver down, then realised I had not asked Randall what he had meant when he had said "is it about last night?". I toyed with the idea of calling him back but dismissed it: Randall probably would not answer anyway.

What to do next? I drummed my fingers on my desk in frustration for a minute or so, then picked up the phone once again and asked Janet to get hold of Tom Bremner for me.

The phone buzzed. I picked up the receiver. 'Tom?' I started, 'I need to see you as soon as possible.'

Tom's booming voice sounded a little grim. 'And I need to see you too. Wine bar at six?'

I agreed to this and rang off, wondering why Tom had sounded unlike his normal, jovial self.

The rest of the afternoon seemed interminable. I tried ringing Marcus but his phone was switched off. A thought occurred to me and I rang my home.

After a few rings, Freda picked up. As was her way, she answered by saying immediately, 'Who is it?' a habit which I used to find irritating, but now I just try to ignore.

'It's me, Freda. Ben. Is Marcus at home by any chance?'

'Oh, hello, Mr J. No, he went out. He didn't seem quite himself. You want to be careful about Mr Marcus. There aren't that many fish in the barrel, you know. You don't want him leaving.'

'Thank you, Freda,' I replied stiffly, 'I'll burn that bridge when I come to it.'

Dammit, I thought, *she's got me at it now!*

In a fit of truculence, I added, 'In fact, when I get to that river, I'll build a bridge, cross it, then burn it down after me – I am nothing if not thorough,' and slammed the phone down.

I left the office just before six, walked the few yards to the local wine bar, Et Alia, and went in. I looked for Tom in our usual place but he wasn't there, so I ordered a couple of glasses of wine at the bar and took them over to the table. After a minute or so, Tom appeared and plonked his not-inconsiderable frame down next to me. He picked up his glass and muttered, 'Cheers, Ben, I'm ready for this,' and took a hefty swig of wine.

Placing his glass down on the table, he looked at me and said, 'OK, then, what's so important?'

I was about to launch forth when I remembered that Tom had also said he wanted to see me about something. I started to ask him about that, but he waved me impatiently aside.

'Never mind that now, we'll come to it later. Go on.'

Tom was not being his normal self today, but I carried on regardless.

'It's this Ryan Simmons case,' I began. I could see Tom look impatient. I carried on, 'Look, I don't think that he's being truthful about this accident.'

'No?' Tom looked at me hard, 'Why do you say that?'

I held up my hand and starting to tick points off with my fingers.

'Well, point one: why were Ryan and Scott going through the park if they were walking from The Wonk to the taxi rank? It's further that way than going along the road.'

Tom shrugged. 'Go on,' he said.

My forefinger came out. 'Two: Ryan was supposed to have fallen and broken his leg *inside* the park, yet when the ambulance came they were *outside* on the road. That's at least two hundred yards away – a long way to stagger with a broken leg.'

Tom gazed at me. 'Next point,' he barked.

Middle finger now. 'Thirdly, Ryan broke his leg in the accident, certainly. But if he had tripped as he said, then you would have expected damage to his wrists and arms as he fell forward, but there weren't any. Or at least, nothing of any consequence.'

Tom looked into the middle distance for a moment as if considering something, then turned back to me. 'Anything else?'

I hesitated for a second. 'Well, just a feeling when I saw Ryan and his father that they were covering something up.'

Tom pulled a face. 'I see,' he said, 'a feeling, eh? And what are we supposed to do about this feeling?'

I was a bit taken aback. 'We ought to say to the council, or I suppose, the council's insurers, that this claim is probably bogus.'

'But we have no proof of that, Ben!' Tom argued. 'Just some observations and a "feeling"!'

'Well, we could investigate further and find proof,' I said obstinately.

'Oh, come on, Ben, you're not Inspector Lestrade of the Yard! And anyway, then what?' asked Tom. 'Have you thought through the consequences?'

I just looked at Tom mutely.

'Well then, I'll tell you,' Tom went on remorselessly, 'Ryan, who not only has broken his leg, and lost God knows how much in income because he can't work, could well be charged with fraud. This on top of his wife leaving him and him having to move in with his father. Scott and Patrick could also be charged with fraud, or even perjury if this went to court. They could all end up in clink. Added to which, you and I could say goodbye to our fees! And it really is not your job to do this – all you were asked to do was work out a few figures!'

I was getting angry now. 'But there is such a thing as ethics!' I protested, 'I have a duty, and my moral compass tells me…'

'Oh, you and your moral compass!' Tom scoffed, 'you seem to have been using that particular device a lot recently, haven't you? Marcus said you'd produced it to him last night. You can be such a prig at times, Ben. No wonder, Marcus…' his voice trailed off and he looked as though he had said more than he had intended.

'No wonder Marcus what?' I asked.

I was starting to get uneasy now: it suddenly came back to me that Randall Barratt had prefaced our conversation earlier with an odd reference to the previous evening.

Tom looked down at his feet for a moment, then said, 'That's why I wanted to talk to you. About Marcus. And you.'

'Go on,' I prompted. 'Obviously something happened last night.'

Tom nodded. 'Yes. Marcus came in here and he'd clearly had a few drinks somewhere.'

'Probably at the squash club,' I interjected. 'He said he had a match.'

Tom continued, 'Well, he came in here – don't know whether he was looking for you – but anyway, by chance, that prat Randall was here too, with some of the people from CAOS.'

There was a pause whilst Tom took another gulp of wine before he went on. 'So anyway, Marcus made a beeline for Randall, and I don't know what they said to each other, but there was some sort of altercation and the next thing is, Marcus has plonked himself down next to me and is crying on my shoulder. I mean, literally crying.'

'And…?' I prompted him again.

'And it all came out. That you'd had an argument, that you didn't want to go to New York with him and that all you were bothered about was your friggin' moral compass. Or words to that effect.' Tom had another gulp of wine. 'And so I gave him a glass of wine – that might have been a bit of a mistake when I think about it, because he'd already had a few, but what the hell? Then I escorted him to your front door. I would have talked to you then, but there were no lights on, so I thought I'd better leave it.'

'Oh hell!' I said, 'Look, I'd better explain.' I quickly told Tom about what had happened the previous evening before Marcus had slammed out of the house.

'So you see, Tom, all I said was that I have to be with my family at Christmas and that they come first.'

Tom snorted. 'Very right and proper, Ben. I agree. But there are ways of doing and saying things like that. Don't forget, Marcus doesn't have much in the way of family – a sister he sees about once a year and a couple of nephews ditto – and I think he feels vulnerable. If it seems that you're trying to push him away as well, then perhaps no wonder he got upset. Couldn't you have been a bit more understanding?'

I pulled a face. 'Oh, I suppose so. I didn't mean to be so harsh. And I suppose he's had a few drinks, then said something a bit flirty to old Randall, who has taken it the wrong way. No wonder Randall sounded a bit wary when I spoke to him.'

Tom raised an eyebrow, so I told him of my conversation with Randall earlier that afternoon.

Tom said, 'Look, Ben, I'm very fond of you both, but there are times when I could bang both your heads together. You need to talk and sort things out. You should have done that last night, you know!' Here he wagged a finger at me in admonishment. 'My mother always used to say "Don't let the sun go down on a disagreement" and she's quite right!'

I had to acknowledge the truth of all this, so nodded assent. 'Yes, OK, I will talk to him.'

Tom nudged me and said, 'Well, here's your chance!' and indicated the door, where Marcus had just appeared, before squeezing my arm and adding, 'I'll leave you to it.'

I said, 'Yeah, thanks, Tom. But before you go, what about the Simmons case?'

Tom gave a rueful laugh. 'You're like a dog with a bone sometimes, young Ben. All right, I'll think it over and call you tomorrow. OK?' He disappeared in the direction of some of his cronies who were standing at the bar.

Marcus appeared by my side a second later. 'Can I sit there?' he indicated the chair next to mine.

'Of course,' I replied and he lowered his six foot-two frame onto the seat. There was a slight pause then we both began to speak at once.

'Look…' I began.

'Ben, I'm sorry…' Marcus started.

We both stopped, but I indicated to Marcus to carry on.

He said. 'Actually, you have Freda to thank for me being here, really.'

I expressed surprise. 'Freda? Why?'

Marcus grinned. 'Well, I was looking a bit glum earlier and when she asked what was the matter, I said that I thought you didn't want me around anymore. And she said, "Oh, I think you're barking up the wrong dog, there, Mr Marcus, he still holds a candle to you!"'

I laughed. 'By which, I take it she meant that you're wrong and that I still carry a torch for you!'

Marcus nodded. 'And then she gave me a right bollocking and told me not to be so stupid and to go and make it up with you straightaway. So here I am. So do you?'

'Do I what?'

'Still carry a torch for me?'

I gave a snort, 'Yes, of course I do, you chump! And a candle! But,' I added in a confidential tone, 'not a friggin' moral compass!'

Tom joined us after a while. 'All well now?' he asked in a slightly apprehensive tone. He looked relieved when we assured him that it was, and said, 'Well, thank God for that!'

We told him that we had decided I would go with Marcus to New York but we would be back home for Christmas itself.

'Though how I'm going to get that past Janet, I don't know,' I said ruefully. 'And I'll have to make sure the office Christmas party is done and dusted before we go. Unless I can persuade her to leave it until January...'

'So everything's good?' asked Tom.

Marcus agreed, but added, 'Apart from the fact that I haven't come up with a name for this product yet.'

'Oh, I thought of one the other day,' I interjected. 'Now, let me see, what was it. I made a note on my phone.' I fumbled in my pocket and produced my phone. 'Ah, yes, here it is. "Gloxinole". How about that?'

If I was expecting a rapturous round of applause, I was sadly disappointed. The others looked underwhelmed, to say the least. 'Well, I like it,' I said in an injured tone. 'It certainly licks all the other suggestions we've had.'

Marcus suddenly leapt up and said, 'That's it! You're brilliant, Ben! Sorry, must dash,' and with that, hurried out of the wine bar, calling as he went 'See you later, Ben.'

Tom and I were left staring at each other in surprise. 'What was all that about? I thought he didn't like the name!' I exclaimed.

Tom said, 'Well, perhaps it just took a few moments for it to sink in. Anyway, he seems pleased, so that's something. I think now there's only one thing for it – another glass of wine, Ben?'

The next day at the office, I had to break it to Janet that the date of the Christmas party would have to be moved this year. Normally, we have it on a Friday evening the week before Christmas itself, to give everyone time to recover. But as this was the same time that I had agreed to go to New York, this would have to be altered.

Janet looked less than impressed.

'Well, we could have it without you, I suppose,' she mused, lips compressed.

'No way,' I protested, 'there's no telling what the bar bill would get to if I didn't keep an eye on things.'

'Yes, I suppose you do add a sort of baleful presence,' she said tartly. 'A bit like Banquo's ghost at the feast.'

And that would make you Lady Macbeth, I thought a bit irked by this.

Out loud I said, 'And we haven't yet decided on a venue. I had a look at The Wonk but it's no good. It did give me an idea though.'

'The Metropole, like Mr Bremner's firm?' she asked eagerly.

'Well, no' I said carefully, 'I think the Metropole is a bit...er...flash, don't you?'

And also too flippin' expensive, I thought, but hurried on before she had time to respond. 'No, I wondered about The Manor House. They have a nice room there and it's a bit more sophisticated than some places.'

Also, it's owned by Bill Wainwright, like The Wonk, and I could probably get a discount, I thought to myself.

Janet considered this. 'We'd have to provide taxis for everyone –it's a bit out of town, isn't it?'

I was forced to concur. 'And the other thing I thought,' I continued, 'we could have it in January, after the Christmas rush. The staff would probably prefer that – it wouldn't interfere with all their other Christmas parties.'

And also it would be cheaper in January, I could have added, but didn't.

Janet's lips went even thinner. 'And we would have a proper disco?' she asked, giving me one of her gimlet looks.

I was prepared for this and made a show of reluctant agreement.

'And a karaoke?' she added, giving the gimlet a final thrust.

'Why not?' I said in a bright tone, though in actuality, I could think of many good reasons why not...

Mid-morning, the phone went and Janet announced Tom wanted to speak to me. She put him through, and Tom's voice boomed out on my speaker-phone, causing the pens on my desk to rattle.

'Get yourself over to my office at two pm, will you, Ben? I've been thinking over what you said and so I've got Ryan and his father coming in to see me. I want you to be there as well. OK?'

'Sure,' I replied, 'I'll see you then.' I couldn't resist adding, 'Moral compass swinging a bit then, eh?'

I received a snort in response and the line went dead.

I duly made my way down the high street to Tom's offices, which comprise a fine double-fronted Georgian townhouse, behind which had been cunningly added a large extension to accommodate his apparently ever-increasing empire. Although Tom had asked me to present myself at two, Simmons' father and son were not due until two-thirty. 'Gives us half an hour to get our act straight,' as Tom put it.

Two-thirty arrived, and Ryan and Patrick were ushered in to Tom's rather magnificent office with its graceful bow window and panoramic view down the high street. Tom stood up behind his enormous desk and gestured to the pair to sit down.

'Of course, you know Ben, don't you?' he said, waving a hand vaguely in my direction.

The two shot me looks, but nodded agreement. Tom went on suavely, 'I asked Ben to sit in on this meeting, so that he is fully up to speed, and in case anything comes to light which might affect his report.'

Patrick spoke first. 'But why are we here? I thought everything was done as far as we are concerned.'

Tom gave a grimace and said, 'Well, we thought that was the case, but it has been suggested that the council's insurers might want to make a bit of a fight of it.' Tom omitted to mention that so far *he* was the only one suggesting it.

'You mean we might have to go to court?' Ryan cut in.

Tom looked over his half-moon glasses in a magisterial fashion. 'There is always that possibility,' he affirmed, 'and so I want to make sure that we all are singing from the same hymn-sheet, to coin a phrase, before this thing goes any further.'

Patrick Simmons bristled. 'It's all in our statements,' he said in an impatient tone. 'There's nothing further to say.'

Tom gave him a half smile. 'Very possibly, Mr Simmons, but perhaps it would be as well to consider how, for instance, the insurers would look at it. And of course, it is Ryan that would be in the firing line, in a manner of speaking.'

All eyes turned toward Ryan, who was staring fixedly at the carpet. Tom went on, 'So let's start should we? Ryan, how did that evening begin?'

Ryan looked up. 'Well,' he said, 'Scott came round to ours, then we decided to go into town for a couple of beers. Dad here said he'd give us a lift in, but he was going somewhere himself later so we'd have to make our own way home.'

I chipped in, 'And how many beers did you, in fact, have at The Wonk...er...I mean The Black Horse?'

Ryan hesitated for a moment.

Tom said, 'Remember, there were plenty of other people, including the landlord, who could be asked how much you had.'

Ryan shrugged. 'I suppose so. I don't know, but it must have been four or five. My wife had just left me and Scott was trying to help me get over it,' he added defiantly.

I nodded sympathetically. 'Of course. It must have been a trying time for you.'

Tom chipped in, 'And I suppose, after four or five or so pints, one might say you were possibly a little...er...convivial, shall we put it? I'm merely suggesting this is what might be put to you by the insurers,' he added, noting the expressions on the faces of Simmons' *père et fils*.

Taking my cue from a slight nod of Tom's head, I continued. 'And they may also ask why when you and your good friend Scott went in search of a taxi, you went through the park, which is a considerably further route than going down the road.'

Ryan said stubbornly, 'I already told you, we were talking so much we didn't notice where we were going.'

'And they might also have noticed that if you went along the road, instead of through the park, there is a brick wall, which gets to about five feet high. And they might just think: "Oh, here are two young men, full of good cheer, walking along, see a wall and think it would be good fun to run along the top." And they might just say, "Well, after four or five pints of beer, walking along the top of a wall, in the dark, on a cold and frosty January evening, it is *just* about possible that one of them fell off."' I paused, whilst Ryan went ashen and turned towards his father.

Patrick, however, was made of sterner stuff. 'There was a hole in the path in the park. The council found it and repaired it.' He folded his arms and glared at me.

Tom said smoothly, 'True, but they couldn't say how long the hole had been there, could they? And of course, it would be an easy matter for *someone* to make a hole or enlarge an existing one, particularly if they had access to building tools. And a bit of experience.' He paused for a few seconds. 'And am I right in thinking that Ryan took over *your* building business, Mr Simmons.'

Tom turned to me and said, 'Perhaps we should leave Messrs Simmons for a few moments, Ben, so that they can have a little chat between themselves.'

We both got up and walked towards the door. 'Back in ten,' Tom called breezily over his shoulder as we left.

It was quite a gathering later that day in Et Alia. Tom and me, of course, celebrating the conclusion of the Simmons case, Janet, who for once had decided to let her hair down, old "Creepy" Crawley and some of his team (including, I was interested to notice, Alice in Ledgerland) not forgetting Marcus, who arrived looking extremely pleased with himself. Not two minutes after the latter had made an appearance, I was astonished to see none other than "Freda-wot-does" stumble in.

'Hello, Freda, what brings you here?' I asked, 'I thought The Wonk was your usual watering-hole.' I turned to the assembled company and said, 'Hey, everyone, this is Freda.'

Freda looked round. 'Evening, each,' she said, then turning to Marcus, 'Here, Mr Marcus, I dashed after you because you left your wallet and phone on the hall table.'

Marcus thanked her profusely. 'Come on, now you're here, join us for a drink. What'll you have?'

'Oh, well, why not?' replied Freda, 'I'll have one of those penis coladas.'

'Better make it a stiff one!' I heard Tom mutter as he signalled to the barman.

A little later, when we were sitting in our usual corner and Creepy and his team had moved over to the bar, I turned to Freda and said, 'I'm glad you're here actually, because it was thanks to you that Tom and I have been saved some embarrassment.'

Freda looked quizzical so I swiftly explained, without mentioning names, the details of the Simmons case.

'And,' I concluded, 'it was you saying that it was a funny way to go to the taxi rank that first made me wonder.'

'So what happened in the end?' asked Janet.

'Well, Ryan couldn't keep up the pretence,' I replied. 'In fact, it wasn't even really his idea. It was Patrick, when he went to the hospital that night, who suggested that it would be better to say that Ryan had tripped and try to get some compensation out of the council.'

'And did it all happen as you thought? I mean, was he walking along the wall and fell?' asked Marcus.

I shrugged. 'Well, yes. And it turns out that Patrick had made a claim a few years ago for something similar – I mean tripping on a pavement – and got a few thousand from the local authority. I suppose that was what gave them the idea to try it on this time.'

'And it may well have worked, except for you, Ben,' chipped in Tom.

I tried to look modest. 'Possibly,' I said, 'although in fact I wonder if there might have been more of an investigation by the insurers if we had gone ahead. We probably did them no favours by bumping up the claim to about three times what it was originally – all perfectly justified, of course. Creep…er… I mean Alex there did a great job of preparing the loss claim. And if it had been a bona fide case, it would have been a great result. But I suppose there was more chance of the insurers taking a harder line with the larger sums at stake.'

'What'll happen to them now?' Marcus enquired. I turned to Tom. 'Your call on this one, I think.'

Tom took a swig of wine. 'I am hopeful that it will all just fade away. We may have to do a bit of ducking and diving, but as the insurers have not actually paid any money out, I think they will be relatively happy just to drop it. The times they have pursued people for this type of thing is usually when they have already shelled out a wad of money in compensation, and they're trying to claw it back.'

'So all's well that ends well!' said Janet.

I pulled a face. 'Not sure that my bill's going to get paid. I don't suppose I'm flavour of the month with those two at the moment.'

'Never mind,' said Janet robustly, 'I have some good news. Firstly, I've booked The Manor House for the office party!'

'Great!' I tried to sound enthusiastic, 'and secondly?'

'I've chosen the song we're going to do in the Christmas show. I've put us down to do Sonny and Cher's *I've Got You, Babe*. It'll be great!'

I opened my mouth to protest at this unilateral decision, but then thought better of it. Time still to argue the toss…

'And I have good news too,' Marcus put a hand on my shoulder. 'The name for the mouthwash. The Board loved my idea. Well, in fact, *your* idea, Ben.'

'What? You mean "Gloxinole"?' I was a bit surprised.

Marcus looked impatient. 'No, not bloody "Gloxinole", you oaf! I mean "Licksall".'

'Did I come up with that?' I didn't recall it.

'Course you did!' Marcus nudged me, 'You said "it licks all the others" and I suddenly thought, "Bingo! That's it. Job done!"'

'Well, I'm glad I was of service,' I replied with a mock bow.

'And,' Marcus was in full flow now, 'I've booked your flight to New York. Same flight as the rest of us.'

'I presume I'll have to pay for it though?' I asked.

'Yes, but it's in economy, so not too pricey.'

'Fair enough,' I said, then a thought struck me, 'Just a sec, I thought your lot always went business class?'

Marcus looked sheepish. 'Yes, we do. But I'll come through and talk to you.'

'Wonderful,' I said with a heavy dose of irony.

It occurred to me that I was shelling out for my own office party, then paying to go to Marcus's party, with the added treat of being on my own in steerage on the journey.

I sighed, but lifting up my glass said, 'Oh well, a bit early I know, but Merry Christmas, one and all!'